THE

ELIXIR'S

CURSE

A Life Eternal, A Fate Unforgiving

ECHO SABLE

Table of Contents

CHAPTER 1

The Last Request

The air was crisp with the promise of spring, a perfect day for exploration and escape. My mind was set on the journey ahead, the allure of unfamiliar roads calling like a siren. Yet, as dawn broke, the phone shattered the morning calm. It was Jack, the tenacious head of the police task force. He informed me that someone had requested my presence—Brian Xi.

Ordinarily, I might have dismissed any such request or postponed it until after I returned. But Brian Xi was no ordinary man. With mere hours remaining until his execution, his story demanded immediate attention. By four o'clock this afternoon, the world would lose him.

His fate was no secret; it was splashed across every newspaper headline. Brian Xi, a man condemned for the murder of his own brother, Mark Xi.

The trial had captivated the nation, a case shrouded in mystery and intrigue. Despite his fervent appeals, the courts stood firm, reaffirming the grim sentence.

The enigmatic layers surrounding this case have captivated the public's imagination, transforming it into a sensational narrative. Even I, an outsider with no direct involvement, found myself ensnared by its complexity.

I pored over every newspaper report, seeking clarity amidst the chaos, yet the core of the mystery slipped through my grasp. Without firsthand interaction with Brian Xi, my understanding remained frustratingly superficial.

What truly sets this case apart is its peculiar nature. Brian Xi, by all accounts, had no discernible motive for murder. His actions and circumstances defy conventional logic, rendering the case as baffling as it is intriguing.

Brian Xi was a man of considerable wealth, with an inheritance that spoke volumes of his family's affluence. Yet, his financial prosperity was not what defined him. His younger brother, Mark Xi, had also been destined for a life of privilege until the ravages of World War II intervened. As an officer in the U.S. Army, Mark Xi vanished amidst the chaos of combat, leaving behind a legacy of uncertainty and presumed loss.

In the aftermath, Brian Xi faced a choice that tested the very fabric of familial loyalty. With his brother missing and presumed dead, he had every opportunity to claim the inheritance left behind. But Brian Xi's heart defied such logic; he refused to accept that his brother was gone. Decades after the war's end, his conviction remained unshaken—his brother was alive.

Driven by this belief, Brian Xi embarked on an exhaustive search, dispatching teams to scour the islands of the South Pacific. His quest was no secret; it was a testament to his relentless hope that resonated throughout society. Expeditions received his funding with a single stipulation: uncover Mark Xi's fate.

The Pacific Island battles of World War II had been among the most harrowing, claiming countless lives. The prospect of locating one man amid such devastation seemed impossibly remote, akin to finding a needle in a haystack. Friends and advisors urged Brian Xi to abandon his quest, but he remained resolute. The bond with his brother, forged in childhood, was a beacon, guiding him through the darkness.

Brian Xi's unwavering determination and the sincerity of his mission caught the attention of the U.S. military. In a remarkable gesture, they granted him access to wartime records, refining his search parameters and offering a glimmer of hope.

And then, against all odds, the impossible happened—a miracle. Brian Xi found his brother. The reunion was not merely a testament to his relentless pursuit but a profound affirmation of faith, resilience, and the enduring power of familial love.

Finally, in an extraordinary twist of fate, Brian Xi's unwavering hope was rewarded—he found his brother. Their miraculous reunion reverberated across society, captivating the public's imagination. Yet, the jubilation was short-lived, as the story took a tragic turn that no one could have anticipated.

Merely three days after their return, the headlines erupted with even more astonishing news: Brian Xi had murdered his brother. Witnesses claimed he pushed Mark Xi off a cliff, with at least seven people observing the act and twenty more hearing the victim's piercing scream echoing through the canyon. Despite exhaustive searches, Mark Xi's body was never recovered—experts surmised it had been swept away by the relentless tides.

After the horrific act of pushing his brother down the hill, Brian Xi stood in stunned silence, as if frozen in time. It wasn't until the police arrived and clasped handcuffs around his wrists that he stirred from his trance.

In the ensuing legal whirlwind, Brian Xi maintained an eerie silence, offering no defense against the charges. Despite his wife's efforts to assemble a formidable legal team, even the most skilled attorneys found themselves impotent in the face of overwhelming evidence.

Seven witnesses had seen the crime unfold, their testimonies painting a damning picture. Moreover, three renowned neurologists and psychologists testified with unwavering certainty that Brian Xi was of sound mind and fully aware of his actions.

The courts delivered a swift verdict — death. Yet, the question lingered like a shadow: what was Brian Xi's motive? For a man of his intellect and education, the act of murdering his own brother demanded a rationale, a logic that eluded even the most seasoned investigators.

He had devoted his life to finding Mark Xi, expending vast resources and time in the search. Could it be that he brought his brother back only to commit such an unthinkable act? If so, was he mad? But the experts had been unequivocal—Brian Xi was no lunatic.

This enigma drew me deeper into the case, compelling me to gather every piece of information I could find. Brian Xi's silence left a void that was filled by his wife, Ms. Luna Xi. Her interviews painted a poignant picture of a man driven by devotion, recounting the exhaustive efforts and joy that accompanied the brothers' reunion.

Ms. Luna's detailed accounts bolstered the argument of her husband's innocence, portraying him as a man incapable of such betrayal. Yet, her heartfelt defenses could not alter the grim outcome. The mystery of Brian Xi's motive remained, an unanswered question that haunted the corridors of justice and intrigued all who dared to ponder its depths.

At the time, I had a theory that seemed to fit the puzzle. My inference was that Brian Xi hadn't brought back his brother from the deserted island, but rather an impostor. Perhaps, upon realizing this, Brian Xi was driven to a moment of madness, leading him to kill the man he had returned with.

However, this theory quickly unraveled. Every piece of evidence confirmed that the man Brian Xi brought back was indeed Lieutenant Mark Xi, the missing American military officer. Fingerprints and facial recognition matched; there was no doubt of his identity. Thus, the motive behind Brian Xi's deadly act remained an inscrutable mystery.

I had resigned myself to the idea that this enigma would remain forever unsolved. That was until the police contacted me with unexpected news: Brian Xi wanted to see me, just hours before his execution.

I was no luminary in the world of crime-solving, merely an ordinary individual with a knack for unraveling the complex and bizarre. Brian Xi's request to see me suggested that he harbored a burden that needed addressing, a truth that eluded everyone else.

Without hesitation, I agreed to meet Jack, abandoning my travel plans. Whatever compelled Brian Xi to reach out at such a critical moment was bound to be significant, and I felt an undeniable pull to uncover the truth that had eluded us all.

In Jack's office, I found myself once again face-to-face with the seasoned police officer with whom I'd had many spirited debates. He greeted me with a mix of sarcasm and camaraderie, arms wide open, "Welcome, welcome, you are the savior of the dying."

Though his words were tinged with dissatisfaction, I met them with a calm smile. "I think Brian Xi might be a bit off to think I'm some kind of pastor," I quipped, trying to lighten the mood.

Jack, however, was in no mood for humor. "I don't know what he thinks you are, but time's running out. Let's go see him," he said tersely.

Together, we left the police station and made our way to the prison. The scene outside was chaotic, with journalists swarming the entrance, hoping to grasp any new development. Inside, the atmosphere was no less intense, resembling a legal conference more than a penitentiary.

Top lawyers from across the city, summoned by Ms. Luna, were tirelessly working to secure a stay of execution and prepare for another appeal. Their efforts, it seemed, had begun to bear some fruit.

In the prison's reception room, I encountered Ms. Luna for the first time. Her photographs didn't quite capture the delicate, almost fragile presence that she projected in person. Pale and poised, she sat listening intently to a lawyer's counsel, her demeanor betraying the heavy weight of her sorrow.

As Jack and I entered, someone whispered in her ear, prompting her to rise and approach me. Her movements were graceful, reflecting her education and restraint, and her composure under such duress elicited an instinctive sympathy.

"Mr. Morris?" she asked softly, her voice barely above a whisper.

I nodded, "Yes, I am Ash Morris."

Her smile was a painful acknowledgment of the situation. "I'm sorry to trouble you. He refused to see anyone, not even me, yet he asked for you."

Initially, a sense of unease lingered within me, but as Luna spoke, any trace of irritation dissipated. Her words conveyed the urgency and desperation with which Brian Xi sought my assistance. It was clear that his request wasn't made lightly, and that only deepened my resolve.

As the central figure in such a perplexing case, Brian Xi's decision to reach out to a stranger like me, especially when he wouldn't even see his own wife, suggested that he had compelling reasons for doing so. This was not a plea made on a whim; it was a call for help from someone who found themselves in the darkest of circumstances.

"Please, there's no need for formalities, Mrs. Xi," I responded quickly, understanding the weight of the moment. "I will do everything in my power to help him."

Tears glistened in her eyes, her voice trembling with conviction. "Thank you, Mr. Morris. I believe in his innocence."

In such a heavy moment, words of comfort eluded me, and with Jack's persistent urging, I found myself moving forward swiftly.

The path to the death row cell was a gauntlet of security, each layer more formidable than the last. As we navigated through the prison's fortified corridors, the atmosphere grew heavier. We finally reached Brian Xi's cell. At Jack's presence, a jailer promptly pressed a button, and the door swung open with a metallic clang.

The cell was dimly lit, casting long shadows that seemed to stretch endlessly. Jack gestured for me to proceed, his direction simple and unyielding, "You go in."

Stepping inside, I found nothing remarkable about the cell itself; it was as nondescript as any other around the world. But as the door closed behind me, sealing me inside, my focus shifted entirely to the man before me—the enigmatic figure at the heart of this confounding case.

Brian Xi and Luna were indeed a pair that complemented each other perfectly. Despite his frail appearance and pallor, he exuded an air of gentleness and intellect, a scholarly aura that belied his circumstances. His face had a certain elongation, and there was a brightness in his eyes that spoke of both sanity and intelligence. Seated on the prison bed, he gazed at me with wide, searching eyes.

For a moment, silence reigned as we regarded each other, the weight of unspoken words hanging in the air. Finally, he broke the silence, his voice tinged with a curiosity that matched his gaze. "You, are you the person I want to see?"

I nodded, taking a seat beside him on the bed. The silence stretched once more, but this time it was I who could not endure it. "Don't waste your time," I said bluntly, breaking through the quiet with a directness borne of urgency. The clock was ticking, and whatever he needed to convey, whatever truth he wished to share, the time for revelation was now.

He stood up abruptly, stepping closer until he was leaning over me. His voice was clear and unwavering as he uttered the words, "Help me escape!"

The request was as simple as it was astounding, leaving me momentarily speechless. It was the most shocking plea I'd ever encountered. "Do you know what you're saying?" I asked, trying to digest the enormity of his words.

He nodded emphatically, "I know, I know. I realize it's a little late to ask you this."

His choice of words puzzled me. He didn't describe his request as "excessive," just "a little late." The implication eluded me, and I struggled to grasp what was running through his mind.

I fixed him with a steady gaze, and he continued, "But there was no other way. Only at the last moment did I feel I could trust you enough to ask for your help. You've accomplished things others deemed impossible, so naturally, you can help me escape from this prison."

I sighed, feeling the weight of his anticipation. It was a moment that required me to reassess everything I thought I knew about his mental state.

"I know over 700 ways to escape from prison," I replied, my tone measured. "And I've known experts in the art of escape—people for whom no prison is impenetrable."

His eyes lit up with hope. "So you'll help me?"

I gave a wry smile, tempered by the reality of his situation. "Whether I agree or not is beside the point. In your current circumstances, escape is virtually impossible."

"Why?" he pressed, urgency creeping into his voice. "They're not watching me that closely."

I sighed again, trying to convey the gravity of the situation. "Escaping from prison isn't a simple task. It requires meticulous planning, often spanning years. And you—"

I hesitated, not wanting to continue down a path that led nowhere. Instead, I glanced at my watch, letting the gesture speak for itself.

He should have understood the meaning behind my action. It was a silent reminder that he had a mere three hours and forty minutes left. Realistically, he had even less time, maybe two hours at most. Soon, the chaplain, jailers, and warden would converge, leaving him with no opportunity to escape. His window was closing, and the reality of his predicament was inescapable.

My mind was consumed with a singular question: Why was he so desperate to escape? His escape seemed utterly impossible, yet the urgency in his plea was undeniable.

As I watched him, his pallor deepened, and he twisted his fingers with such force that his knuckles emitted a sharp cracking sound. His voice rose to a near shriek, "No, I must escape!"

"Why?" I pressed, hoping for a glimpse into his reasoning.

"Don't ask me why," he retorted, his tone edged with desperation. "I'm begging you—you must help me escape."

Feeling the weight of the impossibility, I stood up, frustration evident in my voice. "I'm sorry, but this is beyond anyone's capabilities. I really can't help. The lawyers your wife hired are working on a stay of execution. If they can secure a two-month delay, there might be hope."

I shook my head, the finality of my words hanging in the air. "But if the stay isn't granted, there's nothing I can do."

Suddenly, he grasped my hand, his grip like ice, sending a shiver through me. "Mr. Morris, please, use these three hours. I must escape. Believe me, I truly must escape. Please, help me!"

His desperation was palpable, yet I could only respond with honesty. "Please believe me too—I truly can't do it."

Brian Xi's face contorted with a mix of anguish and resolve as he whispered to himself, "I killed him. I'm not innocent. I killed him, but... but I had to. Please, help me!"

I knocked hard three times on the cell door, the prearranged signal for my exit. The door swung open, and I quickly stepped back, expecting Brian Xi to make a desperate dash for freedom. But he didn't. Instead, his voice pierced the air, sharp and pleading, "Help me! You must help me. Only you can do it. You can definitely do it!"

His cry reverberated through the prison, a haunting echo that followed me as I retreated, feeling the weight of his desperation. The cell door shut with an unforgiving finality, sealing him away once more.

Outside the cell, I paused, trying to steady myself. Two police officers hurried towards me, their faces a mix of urgency and concern. "Are you okay? Did he hurt you?" they asked repeatedly, their worry apparent.

Brian Xi's cries had ceased, leaving an unsettling silence in their wake. "No, nothing happened. I'm not that easily hurt," I assured them, though his words had left a mark of their own.

"It's dangerous to meet with those about to be executed," one officer noted, "They know they're about to die, and they can do anything."

I offered a bitter smile, acknowledging the truth in their words. Brian Xi's request for me to help him escape was indeed a desperate act, born of a mind willing to entertain the impossible.

As I walked back to the reception room, the air felt heavy with defeat. The lawyers sat around, dejected, their silence more telling than any words. They leafed through their documents with a sense of resignation, the futility of their efforts evident.

It was clear at a glance—there was no hope for a stay of execution. The legal avenues had been exhausted, leaving only the ticking clock and the inevitability of the sentence. The atmosphere was thick with an unspoken understanding that time was running out, and the mystery of Brian Xi's actions might remain forever unanswered.

Though last-minute stays of execution sometimes arrive just as the prisoner is about to face the electric chair, there's often an indication beforehand whether such a reprieve is likely. The lawyers' strategy was built on the same foundation as their appeal: the absence of Mark Xi's body. They argued, "What if he's not dead?"

If Mark Xi were alive, the charge of murder against Brian Xi would fall apart. The legal team seized upon this possibility, crafting their entire defense around this slim hope.

Had the circumstances of the alleged murder been different, this argument might have held more weight.

But Brian Xi was accused of pushing his brother off a cliff that loomed 892 feet high. Seven witnesses testified to seeing the act from a mere five to ten feet away. The defense's eloquent arguments were swiftly dismantled by the prosecutor's pointed question: "Has anyone ever heard of someone surviving a fall from an 892-foot cliff? The ocean below would have carried the body away!"

It was under these circumstances that Brian Xi's death sentence was cemented. Thus, the appeal based on the same premise seemed destined to fail.

As I emerged from the cell, a profound discomfort settled over me. There was an undeniable sense that Brian Xi's actions concealed hidden motives and dramatic twists. I wanted to help him, to unearth and expose this buried truth, but the reality of the situation rendered me powerless. How could I possibly orchestrate an escape with just two hours until his execution?

Burdened by these thoughts, I made my way through the reception room, intent on leaving. But just as I reached the door, a voice halted me, "Mr. Morris, please wait a moment!"

Turning, I saw Mrs. Xi standing there, her expression filled with misery, deepening my own sense of despair. Despite an urge to turn away and leave it all behind, I stayed. "Yes, Mrs. Xi," I replied, maintaining a polite demeanor even as my heart weighed heavy with the gravity of the situation.

Mrs. Xi met my gaze steadily, her voice deliberate as she said, "We all heard his scream."

I responded with a bitter smile, acknowledging the truth of her words. "Yes, it was quite horrifying."

"I know," she continued, "it was a cry of despair." She paused, her insight cutting through the tension. "I also know that he must have asked you for something, and you rejected him."

Her keen understanding, perhaps born from her intelligence or intimate knowledge of Brian Xi, was evident. I nodded, confirming her suspicions. "Yes."

There was no reproach in her response, no words of blame or flattery. Just a quiet sigh. "Thank you for coming to see him."

With that, she turned to leave, and her departure only deepened my unease. I called out to her softly, "Mrs. Xi, do you know what he asked of me?"

She turned back, shaking her head. "Of course, I don't know."

Lowering my voice to ensure only she could hear, I revealed, "He wants me to help him escape, to break out of prison in the last three hours."

Her surprise was evident, but it quickly gave way to her usual composure. "Since he made such a request, there must be a reason."

I nodded in agreement. "Yes, I believe so too, but I'm unable to help."

I spread my hands in a gesture of helplessness, emphasizing the truth of my words.

Mrs. Xi remained silent, her eyes steady as they met mine.

Mrs. Xi embodied determination, the kind of person who refuses to yield until the very last moment. Her unwavering gaze made me feel even more unsettled, and under its weight, I began to question myself: Was I truly powerless in this situation?

It was a question Mrs. Xi might have voiced, but she didn't. Her silence compelled me to confront it internally. Deep down, I knew there were ways—more than three, in fact—that I could leverage my rapport with the police and my brief interaction with Brian Xi to facilitate an escape.

But any method I employed would inevitably link me to the act. Helping a condemned man escape would not go unnoticed, and my involvement would surely lead to imprisonment.

Such an action would mean forfeiting my freedom unless Brian Xi could somehow exonerate himself post-escape. Otherwise, I'd face eighteen years on the run, the statute of limitations for criminal prosecution. The notion of living as a fugitive for nearly two decades was more daunting than any prison sentence.

Moreover, I had a life beyond this dilemma—a life with Flora, my newlywed wife, and a cherished family. Our happiness was a kaleidoscope of joy and contentment, a life I could not fathom abandoning. The thought of leaving Flora to face imprisonment or a life on the run was unthinkable.

No, I couldn't bring myself to sacrifice everything for Brian Xi, no matter the circumstances. Resolutely, I turned my head away, avoiding Mrs. Xi's penetrating gaze, a silent declaration of my decision.

Mrs. Xi let out a weary sigh. "Mr. Morris, thank you, truly. But there's no hope left for him."

I offered her words of comfort, though they felt hollow. "Try not to despair. There's always a chance for probation. If that happens, you can gather evidence for an appeal."

She said nothing in response, simply turned away. I watched as she took a few steps and sank into a chair, her head cradled in her hands, silent and still.

At that moment, Jack approached me. "What's going on? Why does the inmate on death row want to see you?"

I opened my mouth to respond, but Mrs. Xi's gaze met mine, and I quickly changed course. "I'm sorry, Jack. I can't disclose that right now."

Jack shrugged, feigning indifference, but I could see through it. He cared deeply, his displeasure evident from the moment we arrived.

I understood his frustration. Brian Xi had requested to see me, not him, despite Jack's prominent position in the police force. In his eyes, any prisoner's concerns should naturally be directed his way. Of course, he was irritated.

I felt no need to justify myself to Jack. I started to leave, but he trailed behind, pressing further. "Ash, if you're working with the police, you should tell me why Brian Xi wanted to see you."

I was growing annoyed. Jack was a brilliant officer, yet his arrogance often grated on others. I replied curtly, "First, I've never been one to work with the police; second, Brian Xi's fate is sealed—he's on death row. What relevance does he have to the police now?"

CHAPTER 2

Reckless Actions

Jack's persistence was unwavering, his expression growing darker. Yet, he pressed on. "What did he ask of you? Tell me."

We had reached the prison gates, and I paused, meeting his gaze. "Alright, I'll tell you. He wants me to help him escape from prison."

Jack was taken aback. "And what did you say?"

Annoyed, I retorted, "I told him I can't help with an escape. If he needs a pastor to pray for his soul before he meets his end, that's something I can manage."

Most of those words had been mere venting, never spoken aloud to Brian Xi. Jack, however, couldn't discern my anger. He continued, "What was his response?"

I sighed, "Jack, does it really matter what he said?"

Jack hesitated, the weight of my question hanging between us. His persistence wavered for a moment, but the curiosity in his eyes remained undimmed. I turned away, hoping to leave the conversation behind, but Jack's footsteps followed, relentless in their pursuit of answers.

A few steps later, his voice broke the silence again. "Ash, doesn't this case strike you as odd?"

"Of course, it's strange," I conceded, trying to temper my frustration. "But that's no reason to help him escape just to satisfy my curiosity."

Jack's eyes lingered on mine, searching for something unspoken. "If I were in your shoes, I might act differently," he said, his tone laden with implication.

With those words, he pivoted and headed back toward the prison, leaving me standing at the gates, caught in a web of confusion and unease. What was Jack truly suggesting? Was he testing my resolve, or simply venting his own frustrations?

I pondered his words briefly, but quickly dismissed them. I wasn't about to jeopardize everything by crossing that line. Yet, as I walked away, the echoes of Jack's words mingled with Brian Xi's desperate plea and Mrs. Xi's sorrowful eyes, leaving a disquieting residue in my thoughts that refused to fade.

I stopped after twenty steps, finding myself before a small grocery store.

After a moment's hesitation, I went inside and picked up the phone, dialing my home number. Flora answered.

"What if I had to flee, starting now, and run for years?" I asked abruptly.

My question hung in the air, unexpected and jarring. Flora paused, not pressing for details. She knew I wouldn't ask without reason and took a moment to consider. Her answer was simple and resolute: "I would escape with you."

I held the phone, uncertainty gnawing at me. My eyes wandered aimlessly until they settled on Mrs. Xi, emerging from the prison alone. She halted at the gate, glancing up. I hoped to avoid her gaze, but it was too late—our eyes met.

She began walking toward me.

Flora's voice crackled with urgency over the phone. "Ash, why the silence? What's going on?"

Dropping my voice to a whisper, I replied, "Darling, Brian Xi wants me to help him escape from prison."

"Oh my God," she breathed. "He's facing the electric chair. Do you think you can do it?"

"It's possible, but it would mean breaking the law outright. What do you think?"

"Brian Xi is innocent, I believe that. You could hide for a while, and things might settle. I'll be with you. I know you want to help him. Don't worry about me."

As Mrs. Xi entered the grocery store, I quickly said, "If I'm not back in an hour, something's gone wrong. Meet me at the East Railway Station with everything we'll need."

I hung up just as Mrs. Xi approached, my mind a whirlwind of conflicted thoughts. Mrs. Xi had never explicitly asked for my help, leaving me no opportunity to bolster my resolve and refuse. Jack's words played on a loop in my head, challenging me, daring me to act.

And now, with Flora's unwavering support, my agitation only grew.

Mrs. Xi stood before me, her eyes fixed and steady. Her words caught me off guard. "Mr. Morris, when will you start? Time is running out."

I gaped at her, speechless. Before I could formulate a response, she continued, "Don't ask how I know you'll agree. I just do. You're not one to turn away from a life-or-death plea."

Her certainty was both flattering and daunting. "Mrs. Xi, do you understand that helping your husband could put me in an impossible situation for the rest of my life?"

"Of course I know," she replied calmly, "but you've already decided, haven't you?"

Her insight was disarming, and I found myself without words. Mrs. Xi possessed a remarkable composure and understanding, a rare strength amidst chaos.

Resigned, I asked, "Can he drive?"

She nodded. "Yes, he drives very well."

"I won't just help him escape," I declared, "but I'll also uncover the truth behind his case. Once he's out, I need you both to fully cooperate. Can you promise me that?"

"Absolutely," she replied. "We'll escape together, and I'll tell you everything I know. I'll make sure he shares the truth."

I sighed deeply, feeling the weight of my decision. I recognized the folly of my choice, aware of the risks and the law I was about to defy. Yet, the convergence of circumstances propelled me forward.

"I'll be back in an hour. Wait for me," I instructed before striding away with newfound resolve.

At the bus stop, I waited for ten minutes, during which a plan to aid Brian Xi's escape crystallized in my mind.

The bus pulled up with a hiss of air brakes, and I climbed aboard, settling into a seat near the back. For fifteen minutes, the cityscape blurred by, until I finally disembarked and wound my way through a series of shadowy alleys. My destination? A house owned by a most eccentric friend.

This friend was an enigmatic figure, often described as a "criminal mastermind" in jest. Despite this moniker, he was a multimillionaire with hobbies as unique as his personality. While some wealthy individuals might collect rare orchids or raise exotic animals, my friend preferred a different pastime: crafting intricate criminal plans.

His so-called crimes were the stuff of an "armchair strategist"—a mental exercise in hypothetical mischief. To be precise, he reveled in concocting elaborate criminal scenarios on paper. One day, he might draft an ingenious plan to rob a bank; the next, he would devise a scheme to raid the national treasury. By the day after, he could be plotting a meticulously detailed heist of a mail truck. Each scenario was a masterclass in imagination and precision, a testament to his methodical nature, yet none ever strayed into the realm of reality.

His approach to planning was nothing short of meticulous. He would meticulously survey potential sites, craft precise blueprints, and gather all the necessary tools and materials. Yet, when the moment for execution arrived, he never crossed the line into criminality. Instead, he would lock away every component of the plan in a dedicated room, labeling the door with "Plan No. X" or similar titles. During the lulls between schemes, he would revisit the room, immersing himself in the thrill of his hypothetical escapades.

He was indeed a peculiar individual. Despite his fascination with crime, it was likely that he had never broken even the smallest law. Yet, now, I found myself needing to enlist his expertise for a real venture. Only he possessed such a comprehensive collection of resources, saving me the time and effort of gathering them from scratch. It was a necessity that drew me to him, knowing he could provide exactly what I needed without becoming entangled in the aftermath.

Of course, I had no intention of implicating him. During my journey, I meticulously planned to ensure his complete safety once everything was said and done.

I arrived at his peculiar house and pressed the doorbell. True to his love for "committing crimes," his home was just as unconventional. After ringing the bell, a small square on the door slid open—not to reveal a face, but rather a TV camera tube.

His house was outfitted with TV receivers at every turn, and he even wore a miniature TV receiver on his wrist, much like others might wear a watch. With its tiny half-inch screen, it allowed him to see who was at the door from anywhere inside. I leaned in close to the small square, making sure he could clearly see that it was me standing at his doorstep.

His voice crackled through the intercom, brimming with excitement. "It's you! Perfect timing, Ash. My new project needs an assistant like you—you showed up just in time."

I chuckled. "When you hear why I'm really here, you'll definitely think my timing is impeccable. Open up!"

The door swung open immediately, not by human hand, but through radio control. Having visited more than once, I was well accustomed to his eccentricities.

"I'm in room 17 downstairs, hurry up," his voice directed.

"Downstairs" referred to the underground section of his elaborate home. I descended the stairs and reached room 17, where the door opened automatically to reveal the man I came to see: Rafael Valor.

Do not be deceived by his name, which might conjure images of a gallant, romantic hero. In truth, Rafael Valor was anything but admirable. Despite his immense wealth, he exuded an eccentricity that bordered on the comical.

Physically, he possessed an average build, but that was where normalcy ended. His head was disproportionately large, with facial features so tightly packed they seemed to jostle for space—a chaotic mosaic perched atop an unusually long, slender neck. Psychologists often suggest that such a neck is the hallmark of a vivid imagination. If that theory held true, then Rafael Valor was a living testament.

He was lounging on a massive sand tray—a meticulous model of a bustling city. The streets were alive with moving vehicles, each one gliding at a pace true to its type. In his hand, he wielded a slender metal rod.

At that moment, the rod's tip hovered over a prominent building. The model's accuracy was undeniable, and I immediately recognized it as the silver vault of the National Bank.

He glanced up as I approached. "Yes," I affirmed, "it's the most cash-rich spot, but my visit today isn't about robbing a silver vault. It's about rescuing a death row inmate in a race against time."

Rafael Valor froze momentarily, then his face lit up with an almost childlike excitement, his features contorting humorously. "What a brilliant idea! It's so novel. Let's plan it out!"

I knew that revealing my true intent—to actually execute this plan, not just theorize about it—would shock him. So I kept that detail to myself for now.

"We need to prepare quickly," I said, letting a sense of urgency seep into my voice. "Do you have robes that belong to a religious elder?"

"Yes, yes," he replied eagerly, his eyes flickering with a spark of excitement. "I once devised a scheme using Orthodox elder robes."

"And a nylon fiber mask?" I pressed, watching his reaction carefully.

"Of course," he nodded confidently. "I have plenty."

"Then get dressed quickly. Most Orthodox elders have beards—make sure you don't pick a pretty boy's mask!" I teased, urging him on.

Rafael Valor responded with mock indignation, "Come on, do you really think I'd make that mistake?"

Impatient, I pressed, "Hurry up, get into character. I need you back here in ten minutes, tops. Move it!"

He dashed out, excitement in his step, muttering to himself, "Interesting, interesting!"

I stifled a laugh, anticipating his reaction once he realized just how "interesting" things would become.

True to his "first-class criminal" reputation, Rafael Valor returned in under seven minutes. Clad in a black robe with a flat hat perched on his head, a beard mask covering his face, and a large bead necklace with a cross dangling around his neck, he looked the part perfectly.

"Fantastic," I said, grinning. "Let's go."

He froze. "What did you say?"

"Let's go," I repeated.

He spread his hands, bewildered. "Go? Where to? You must be joking."

"Who's joking? We're saving a death row inmate. You've heard the name Brian Xi, right? In two hours, they'll put him on the electric chair, and I intend to get him out."

Rafael Valor's voice shook. "Ash, this is a fantasy. I... I just plan... That's all."

"Not this time. You're in it for real," I insisted. "You'll be safe afterward. Once inside, I'll knock you out with one punch. Imagine tomorrow's headlines: you're the innocent victim, but secretly the mastermind. Isn't that thrilling?"

I was, in effect, "inducing someone to commit a crime," but desperation demanded it. With no one else to turn to, I had to rely on him.

Flattered and intrigued, Rafael Valor hesitated—my words had hit the right chord. People like him thrive on excitement and a touch of madness.

"Then, at least let me understand the whole plan!" he pleaded.

"No need," I replied swiftly. "If you know too much, you might slip. Just remember three things: First, claim I asked you to pose as an Orthodox priest because the inmate requested it. Second, don't resist when I knock you out. Third, when they drag you to the electric chair, declare you're Rafael Valor before they turn on the current."

His eyes widened in shock. "Ah?"

"What's wrong, backing out?" I challenged.

He stammered, "I... I think the plan's not perfect. Let's review it."

I smiled reassuringly. "No time. Perfecting it means missing our chance. The electric chair waits for no one. Let's go!"

I practically bundled Rafael Valor into the car, driving straight to the prison with urgency thrumming through my veins. To my surprise, upon arrival, Rafael Valor managed to walk in on his own, his composure unexpected but welcome.

Inside the prison reception room, little had changed since my earlier visit, though tension hung thicker in the air with Brian Xi's time dwindling rapidly.

Our entrance—especially with an Orthodox priest in tow—drew immediate attention. Every eye turned our way, curiosity and suspicion mingling in their gazes.

I scanned the room for Jack. His absence was a relief. As a high-ranking officer, Jack would see through my ruse in a heartbeat. Having committed to this desperate gambit, failure wasn't an option.

I glanced at Mrs. Xi, offering a silent assurance with my eyes. She knew of her husband's request, so she likely guessed my intentions. Yet, her composed demeanor made my reassurance redundant.

Approaching the warden, I noted his preparations for the imminent execution. Time was slipping away—just over an hour remained. I gestured toward Rafael Valor and addressed the warden. "I visited earlier to see Brian Xi."

The warden acknowledged, "Yes, Colonel Jack brought you."

I nodded. "Brian Xi asked me to bring an Orthodox priest. He wishes to confess. Please allow us to see him."

The warden scrutinized Rafael Valor briefly, then nodded. "Death row prisoners have the right to choose their clergy." He motioned to a guard. "Escort them inside."

We reached the door of the death row cell without a hitch. As the prison guard opened the electric door, Brian Xi looked up, and I announced, "The priest you requested is here." I actually aimed the statement at the guard, just before the door closed behind us.

Inside, I moved swiftly to Brian Xi. "Quickly, take off the prison clothes," I instructed. "Change into the priest's attire and walk out. You can exit the prison directly. Stay calm—I'll be right behind you. There's a car waiting outside; we can escape immediately."

Brian Xi's response was immediate. He began stripping off his prison garb with efficient haste. Just then, Rafael Valor, who had been silent until now, started to protest, "I don't want to—"

His objection was cut short as I delivered a swift punch to his head, rendering him unconscious. I removed his mask and hat, tossing them to Brian Xi.

Positioning myself with my back against the door, I obscured the small viewing hole. I called out loudly, "Brian Xi, take this opportunity to confess to the priest. It's your last chance..." Then, in a whisper meant only for him, I added, "Just walk out and don't look back."

Brian Xi nodded, his hands moving deftly. Within moments, he was dressed as an Orthodox priest, ready to make his escape.

Though Brian Xi was a bit more robust than Rafael Valor, the voluminous black robe, hat, and mask disguised him well enough that he could easily pass for the Orthodox priest. I signaled him to dress Rafael Valor in the prison uniform, while

I employed my ventriloquism skills, mimicking various voices to create the illusion of a confession taking place within the death row cell.

Once everything was set, I whispered, "Now, start yelling at the priest. The louder, the better. Act like you want to drive him away. Understand?"

At first, Brian Xi seemed confused, but realization quickly dawned. He patted my shoulder and said, "I knew you were the right person for this. I can't thank you enough."

Following my lead, Brian Xi shouted, "Get out, I don't want you here! Leave me alone!"

I joined in, raising my voice, "What are you saying? You asked me to bring a priest, didn't you?"

Brian Xi bellowed again, "Get out, both of you! Leave!"

His shouting reached outside the cell, prompting the guard to open the door without our prompting. As soon as it swung open, Brian Xi bolted out as planned, nearly colliding with the guard. I chased after him, pulling the door shut behind me, exclaiming, "Father, please, let me explain!"

This was the most critical moment. Though I closed the door, the guard could still peer through the small window. If he noticed that the prisoner wasn't Brian Xi, the escape plan would unravel.

I had positioned Rafael Valor face-down on the bed, giving the impression of a man lying listless after an outburst. Glancing back, I noted the guard's lack of reaction and felt a wave of relief wash over me.

With Brian Xi leading and me trailing, we hurried through the corridors. Along the way, officers questioned us, "What's happening? Is he trying to harm you?" To which I loudly replied, "He's gone mad! He requested a priest and then drove him away. It's absurd — please, Father, don't take offense." Brian Xi remained silent, making a beeline for the exit while I continued to apologize profusely.

We navigated through the prison with minimal interference. Brian Xi had memorized the car's plate number and headed straight for it, climbing inside as I followed closely. Just as I was about to reach the car, Mrs. Xi called out to me, "Mr. Morris, please wait a moment."

I turned to find Mrs. Xi flanked by several lawyers, police officers, and the warden himself. Clearly, I couldn't reveal that her husband had just escaped. Trying to maintain composure, I stammered, "I'm sorry, I need to take the priest back. My apologies—"

Before I could finish, the roar of an engine behind me snapped my attention back to the car.

To my shock, Brian Xi had started the car and sped off without me. It seemed he had no intention of sticking to our plan of escaping together. For a fleeting moment, I wondered if Mrs. Xi's call had been a deliberate distraction to leave me behind, as the car peeled away at high speed, leaving me in its dust.

Stranded and betrayed, my mind raced. In that instant, standing there felt like the worst possible idea. Avoiding further suspicion, I ignored the gathering crowd at the prison gate and sprinted away, weaving through the streets until I flagged down a streetcar to the train station. By now, over an hour had passed since I'd contacted Flora, and I hoped she was waiting as planned.

At the train station, I found Flora waiting. She approached with a look of concern. "How did it go?"

I was fuming. "Don't ask. I was duped. We need to find somewhere to hide fast. Do you have any ideas?"

Normally, I could think on my feet, but Brian Xi's unexpected betrayal left me seething, clouding my judgment.

Flora considered our options. "We could buy tickets to another city to throw the police off our trail, but stay hidden here. My father's friend owns a large house. We could hide there without anyone noticing."

I hesitated, wary. "You must consider this carefully. My situation is dire. Will he accept us?"

"Without a doubt," Flora replied confidently. "It was through my father's generosity that he found his place in society, rising to fame."

"Then let's move," I urged, adrenaline coursing through my veins.

Together, Flora and I secured two train tickets. We engaged the ticket seller in friendly chatter, ensuring he'd remember us. I was acutely aware that by tomorrow, my photograph would dominate the evening papers. The ticket seller's recollection would be crucial. After Flora made a succinct call to our eminent contact, we waited at the station, hearts racing.

Soon, a car pulled up, driven by an elderly gentleman. As I approached, I hesitated, "Mr. Miller, I don't wish to involve you. If this imposes—"

Before I could finish, Mr. Miller snapped with a surprising vigor, "Young man, if you persist with this nonsense, I'll have you thrown in the cellar!"

I couldn't help but smile at his spirited defiance. Mr. Miller was clearly a man of action, and for now, I had found sanctuary.

The car wound its way into Mr. Miller's estate, a labyrinthine garden veiled in ancient architecture. Each structure whispered tales of lost dynasties, shadows playing tricks amidst the stonework. The grandeur was overwhelming—a fortress where legends were born, where even an army could disappear without a trace.

Though Mr. Miller wished to host us, we gently insisted he retire for the evening.

Once alone, I sank into the embrace of the plush sofa, frustration boiling over. "Darling, Brian Xi has led me astray."

Flora's eyes reflected a blend of empathy and acute curiosity. "What has he done?"

I threw my hands up in exasperation. "He vanished the moment we left the prison gates. Now, not only am I in jeopardy, but Rafael Valor's entanglements have ensnared me even deeper. I helped Brian intending to unravel a peculiar case, yet here I am—empty-handed and forced into hiding."

Flora sighed softly, a sound that seemed to carry ancient wisdom. "Anger will only entrench the problem."

Her words struck like a tuning fork against my turmoil, resonating truth. She was right; I had been reckless. What good was anger now? The path was clear—I had to find Brian Xi.

His capture was my only hope. Returning him to prison wouldn't absolve me, but it might lessen my burden. Given my connections with international law enforcement, there was a chance, however slim, of redemption. But first, I had to locate Brian Xi.

The question remained: where could he be hiding?

CHAPTER 3

"Nineteenth Level"

In the opulent bedroom Mr. Miller had graciously provided, a suite far more luxurious than my own, I paced restlessly. Beneath the tiled bathroom floor, heated pipes ensured warmth, a welcome luxury against the winter chill.

Flora watched my agitation with amusement. "You've been outwitted," she observed. "Why waste energy on anger?"

My determination only hardened. "I have to find Brian Xi!"

With a gentle smile, she urged, "Then go find him. Don't misdirect your frustration at me."

I laughed, squeezing her hand. "You're remarkable. You always know how to lift my spirits with the right words."

Flora's smile was knowing. "This is likely the top story everywhere now. While you're eager to track down Brian Xi, acting rashly won't help. Wait for the dust to settle, then make your move."

I shook my head, urgency pressing at me. "By then, the police might have already caught him."

She gave a skeptical nod. "I doubt it. If he was clever enough to use you and escape without a trace, the police won't find him easily."

I countered, "They could start by investigating his wife."

Flora chuckled softly. "If Mrs. Xi is anything like you describe, she's a staunch ally to her husband."

Her insight struck me. "What are you implying?"

"You've shared enough for me to believe Mrs. Xi was aware of her husband's plans, and likely complicit in his schemes."

Her logic was undeniable. I slapped my forehead in realization. When I saw Brian Xi flee, I missed the opportunity to monitor Mrs. Xi. If the couple were indeed in cahoots, keeping an eye on her could reveal his whereabouts.

But that chance slipped through my fingers. If Flora's hunch was correct, Mrs. Xi would have vanished by now.

To verify, I called the prison, posing as a lawyer seeking to speak with her. The response was a torrent of profanity, ending with, "That woman might be in hell. Go find her there!"

The call ended abruptly, leaving me with the unsettling truth—Mrs. Xi was no longer in prison.

Brian Xi's escape would have thrown the prison into chaos. My inquiry about Mrs. Xi only added fuel to the fire, and I had no one but myself to blame for the backlash.

Flora, ever the voice of reason, suggested, "Let's lie low for a while. Haven't you often lamented your lack of time to read? Mr. Miller's library is extensive. You can finally indulge in that."

I nodded with a rueful smile. "It seems that's the best course for now."

As dusk settled, casting a warm glow across the room, our conversation was interrupted by Mr. Miller's return. He carried with him a hefty stack of newspapers, each heralding the sensational escape of Brian Xi from prison. With a hurried nod, he placed them before us and spoke of the vast search operation underway. The police had deployed an unprecedented network, offering a staggering reward for our capture. "It's best you remain hidden," Mr. Miller advised, volunteering himself as our sole point of contact, save for a maid who couldn't read, ensuring our safety from betrayal.

Once alone, I unfolded the first newspaper, my heart pounding. In bold headlines, the story of Brian Xi's dramatic prison break unfolded: "Stunning Escape: The Protagonist of the Infamous Brother-Killing Case Evades Execution." The article detailed how, at the brink of execution, the authorities discovered an unconscious figure in Xi's place—Rafael Valor, a successful businessmen. Xi had escaped, and it was clear that he had received assistance—from me, Ash Morris.

In the ensuing media frenzy, I was painted as an enigmatic figure. My past collaborations with international law enforcement, dismantling criminal networks and large-scale syndicates, were well-documented, earning me a somewhat favorable reputation. Many speculated that I might have been coerced into aiding Brian's escape under threat, painting a picture of reluctant complicity.

Yet, none of the reports captured the truth—that I had been cleverly deceived into facilitating Brian Xi's escape, a pawn in his intricate game.

The papers also featured comments from Jack, a senior police official, who announced a two million Dollar bounty for clues leading to our capture, with half the sum for information on just one of us. Jack's triumph was palpable in his photograph, his expression smug, a reminder of how his words outside the prison had influenced my fateful decision to help Brian.

After we pored over the stack of newspapers, Mr. Miller reappeared, bearing yet another edition. This one carried a bold headline: "Two Couples Vanish Together." It detailed how everyone associated with me had been summoned for questioning, and our home had been thoroughly searched. Mr. and Mrs. Xi had vanished into thin air, leaving no clues behind. Meanwhile, Rafael Valor, following his interrogation, had been released. His car was later found abandoned on a lonely road leading out of the city, hinting at a hasty escape into obscurity.

To outsiders, these twists made for gripping drama. For me, entangled in this web, it was a surreal nightmare. Our emotions swinging wildly until the crescendo—seeing our home on TV, ransacked by the police.

Our home, a sanctuary Flora and I had lovingly crafted, was being torn apart. I steeled myself, but Flora was overcome. Despite her resilience, she was still human, and the destruction of our home hit her hard.

Her tears welled, and I swiftly turned off the TV. "We'll rebuild," I assured her softly, "everything will be alright."

Flora nodded, tears falling silently, each one a testament to the storm we were weathering together.

Recognizing the urgency of our situation, I understood that this was not the moment for anger or shared sorrow. Action was imperative. I began pacing, my mind racing as I compiled a list of essentials.

First and foremost, I needed comprehensive information on Brian Xi's case. Every detail, every nuance. If I was to remain hidden, I would use this seclusion to delve deeply into the mystery that had ensnared us. With a more intimate understanding of Xi and his wife, I was confident that a thorough analysis would yield insights previously overlooked.

Additionally, I required makeup supplies—tools to alter my appearance and allow me to venture out undetected. Staying cooped up in Mr. Miller's mansion indefinitely was not an option.

The irony of my predicament wasn't lost on me. Here I was, having risked everything for Brian Xi, and now I found myself in this precarious position. The adage "It's hard to be a good person" resonated deeply. Despite my sacrifices, I was left to navigate the fallout of my misplaced trust.

Fortunately, Flora had secured this refuge just in time, sparing us both from an even more precarious situation.

By morning, Mr. Miller had already arrived, having worked swiftly overnight to gather the resources I needed.

As I awoke from a restless dream of confronting Brian Xi, Mr. Miller presented me with a trove of information on the Xi case. This included not just newspaper clippings but also copies of police files — an unexpected and invaluable resource. Whether through connections or considerable expense, Mr. Miller had procured these documents, and I chose not to question his methods.

In addition to the files, he handed me an intriguing item: a small handbag, seemingly ordinary but full of surprises. It was a dual-purpose accessory, functioning as both a men's briefcase and a women's handbag. Within its compact confines lay an array of disguises: three thin outfits and corresponding masks—two for men and one for a woman—allowing me to assume different identities swiftly, even masquerading as a woman if needed.

The bag also contained clever tools for evading pursuit and sowing confusion, reminiscent of a magician's kit. Each item promised to be useful in tricky situations, and I looked forward to employing them when the time was right.

Having fulfilled my requests, I urged Mr. Miller to leave promptly. His safety was paramount, and with Flora and I being fugitives, it was crucial to minimize his exposure to risk.

That day, I immersed myself in the police files, hoping to unearth insights into the enigma of Brian Xi. Yet, as the hours passed, it became clear that my expectations were overly optimistic. The documents were sparse in substance, a reflection of Xi's obstinate silence. Over an arduous 36-hour interrogation, he had offered the police nothing but, "I don't know."

Xi's wife, Luna, proved equally unyielding. Her legal acumen turned the interrogation on its head, highlighting its illegality and leaving the police stymied.

However, amidst the scant details, the report on the police's search of Xi's residence caught my attention. It contained several anomalies—small, overlooked details that could hold the key to unraveling this complex case.

The report provided intriguing details about the mystery surrounding Brian Xi and his brother, Mark Xi. After their long separation, the brothers shared a room upon reuniting, a seemingly natural choice given their bond. However, the discovery of an unusual object in their room piqued my interest—a bamboo tube, about a foot long, containing black particles and a bright red fiber, resembling a makeshift water filter.

Its origins were unclear. While it might have been brought back by Mark Xi from the South Pacific, the enigmatic patterns carved into the bamboo puzzled experts. These designs didn't match any known motifs from the region, adding another layer of mystery.

Beyond this object, the report noted a conspicuous absence of personal belongings attributed to Mark Xi. He returned alone, carrying almost nothing.

Even more perplexing was the disappearance of Brian Xi's diary. Known for his habit of journaling, the diary vanished without a trace following the incident. Given that Brian Xi was apprehended immediately, he had no opportunity to dispose of it after the fact. If he destroyed it beforehand, it suggested premeditation in killing his brother—but what was the motive?

The bamboo tube and missing diary stood out as critical pieces of this puzzle. Another enigma was the vague account of how Brian Xi located his brother. Their sudden joint appearance raised questions. Aside from a yacht lessor's testimony—who rented a high-performance yacht to Brian Xi days before their return—details of their reunion remained obscure.

The public had focused on the emotional narrative of the brothers' reunion, overlooking the peculiar circumstances surrounding it. I was convinced that unraveling the mystery of their reunion held the key to understanding the entire case.

After dedicating an entire day to the investigation, I was not disheartened by the modest insights I had gained. Time was on my side, and as anticipated, these small discoveries laid the groundwork for deeper revelations.

Over dinner with Flora, I finally shared the plan that had been forming in my mind. "I need to get out and take action," I declared.

Flora looked at me, her concern evident. "Where will you go?"

"I intend to search for Brian Xi, but the key lies in unraveling this peculiar case. I need to head to the South Pacific," I explained. "Understanding how Brian Xi found his brother is crucial. It's likely the key to why he killed him."

Her worry deepened, and she asked, "Do you really think you can leave? The police have sealed off all transport routes."

I shrugged, offering a reassuring smile. "Those are just official measures. I have connections — more than a dozen people who know a hundred ways to transport someone unnoticed, without documents or inspections."

Flora let out a soft sigh, her eyes reflecting a mix of concern and determination. "Don't you want me to go with you?" she asked.

I took her hand gently. "If we move together, we double the risk of being caught by the police."

Still worried, Flora suggested, "Then let's depart separately and reunite at the destination?"

I nodded, albeit with a bittersweet smile. "Alright, we'll act independently. I'm the one the police are after, not you. If they catch you, they might let you go since you're innocent. But you must disguise yourself and proceed with caution. We also need different allies to help us leave the country."

Flora's face lit up with relief and excitement. "I'll start preparing then."

I quickly interjected, "I'll handle the arrangements for you."

My initial plan involved finding two separate contacts to facilitate our escape. However, as I reached out to potential helpers, the responses were dishearteningly similar: "Mr. Morris, you're too 'hot' right now. We've received strict warnings and can't assist you. Please understand."

After enduring seven or eight such refusals, my frustration mounted—not at those who turned me down but at Jack, whose influence had clearly orchestrated this blockade.

Desperation creeping in, I made one last call to a man known as "Nineteenth Level." His infamous reputation stemmed from the belief that he could navigate even the deepest layers of trouble. Although I barely knew him, having only met twice, he seemed my last hope.

After multiple attempts, I finally reached him. Upon hearing my name, he paused, then remarked, "Mr. Morris, you're a wanted man worldwide!"

I replied with a wry smile, "I'm acutely aware. I need to get out of here. Name your price, and I'll pay it."

To my surprise, Nineteenth Level dismissed the notion of payment, calling me "family." The irony wasn't lost on me—I had no desire to join him in his metaphorical nineteenth level of hell. But given my predicament, I had no choice but to play along. "Do you have a way?" I pressed.

"You're too 'hot'—" he began, before I cut him off, my patience wearing thin. "I know. Can you help me or not?"

I braced for disappointment, but his response was unexpectedly positive. "I might be able to, but it'll require a unique approach. The police have implemented stringent measures, including fingerprint checks on all departing vessels."

His words made me acutely aware of the challenges Brian and his wife likely faced as well. An idea sparked. "Nineteenth Level, is anyone else seeking your assistance to leave the city?"

His laughter in response was mysterious and hinted at unspoken possibilities, leaving me both curious and hopeful that a solution might be within reach.

Over the phone, I couldn't see Nineteenth Level's expression, but his laughter was telling. He was clearly holding something back.

I pressed him, my voice edged with irritation, "Nineteenth Level, what's so amusing? Did you help Brian Xi and his wife leave the country as well?"

His laughter turned uneasy. "Sir, in your current predicament, it's best not to meddle in others' affairs."

His dismissive tone irked me, but I kept my temper in check. I needed his assistance, and if he agreed to help, I'd see him soon enough. So, I matched his nonchalance with a chuckle. "You're right. What's the plan?"

After a brief pause, he revealed, "The only viable exit is to ship you out as cargo. The police are fixated on people, not freight."

I grimaced at the thought but accepted the necessity. "Whatever it takes, even if I have to be a zombie, just tell me what to do."

He provided me with an address, directing me to meet a man named Ahan, emphasizing the importance of following his instructions to the letter.

"What about you?" I asked. "Aren't we meeting?"

His laughter returned, sly and evasive. "Do we need to meet?"

"Fine, but you'll have to—" I began, but he cut me off, insisting he'd already spent too much time on the call. "Just follow my instructions."

His interruption left me momentarily stunned. The implications were clear: the elusive Nineteenth Level held the key to Brian Xi's whereabouts, and I had to confront him before I departed. He underestimated me, thinking my current predicament made me vulnerable. A grave miscalculation on his part.

Hanging up, I steeled myself, applying makeup with swift precision, each stroke a battle cry. I slipped out through the back door of the sprawling Miller mansion, my exit as silent as a shadow.

The number I dialed belonged to an exclusive club, a clandestine haven where the world's elite gambled fortunes.

He wouldn't be able to brush me off so easily in person. I was determined to get the answers I needed, no matter the cost.

As I left the Miller residence, I navigated the streets with a newfound confidence. My disguise was impeccable, transforming me into a distinguished middle-aged gentleman, ensuring that no one gave me a second glance amid the bustling city.

The chatter about Brian Xi's escape was omnipresent, a topic on everyone's lips. Even the streetcar driver couldn't resist sharing his so-called "exclusive insights," and I nodded along to maintain appearances.

Upon arriving at the club, I positioned myself strategically by the entrance.

Moments later, two sleek, opulent vehicles pulled up, and two elegantly dressed individuals emerged. Seizing the opportunity, I stepped forward with a confident wave, my voice carrying just the right mix of familiarity and cheer. "Hey, long time no see!"

Caught off guard, they exchanged glances, unsure of whom I was addressing. But their uncertainty worked in my favor; they both offered polite smiles and nodded in acknowledgment. With a measured stride, I seamlessly joined their company, slipping past the threshold into the heart of the club, where secrets and fortunes lay in wait.

Familiar with the club's layout, I headed straight for the roulette room, knowing it was Nineteenth Level's preferred haunt. His boisterous shouts confirmed his presence, a telltale sign of a winning streak. He was engrossed in his game, oblivious to my approach until I placed a firm hand on his shoulder.

His initial glare melted into confusion as I leaned in and whispered, "I'm Ash Morris. If you don't want trouble, come with me."

His reaction was dramatic, feigning indignation. "You want me to follow you now? I'm on a roll! Let me finish three more bets."

I shook my head firmly. "No."

"Two more, one?" he pleaded, desperation creeping into his voice.

"No," I reiterated, "If you don't come now, you're headed for the nineteenth Level of hell."

Resigned, he sighed and rose, following me into a quieter lounge. Once there, he attempted to assert himself. "Don't push your luck. If we cause a scene, it won't end well for you."

I countered with a cold smile, revealing my bluff. "I'm carrying a special gun. It fires a poison-tipped needle that won't kill, but it will paralyze. Want to test it?"

He sat down, his bravado fading. "I'd rather not, thanks."

"Good," I said, pressing him. "Where did you send Brian Xi and his wife?"

"I haven't seen them," he stammered.

Ignoring his denial, I started counting ominously. "One... two... three..."

"Wait, wait," he interrupted. "How high are you counting?"

My voice was icy. "How high do you think I'll go?"

He spread his hands in exasperation. "This is unwise. You know I'm your only way out of the country, yet you're treating me like this!"

"I want the truth about Brian Xi and his wife's whereabouts. You have ten seconds."

Impulsively, I slapped him twice—a rash decision I would later regret deeply.

Clutching his face, he finally relented. "Alright, alright, they left yesterday. They were packed as cargo, marked as cotton fabric, and shipped on the S.S. White Camel."

"Where's their destination?" I inquired.

"Timor Island," he revealed.

I took a deep breath, realizing that Timor Island was also my destination. Situated in the South Pacific, it served as a gateway to numerous islands in the region. However, a pressing question gnawed at me: Why were they heading to the South Pacific once again?

Standing up, I declared, "Alright, I'm going to find that person. Ensure my safe exit, or you'll face the consequences. Remember that."

I turned and walked away without giving him another glance. Exiting the club, I quickly spotted the man I was supposed to find, courtesy of the 19th-Level tip-off. A gaunt figure emerged from the shadows and introduced himself as Mr. Wang. He approached me with a promise to make the necessary arrangements.

"Follow me," he said, his voice barely above a whisper. He led me through the labyrinthine alleys to the vicinity of the pier, a place shrouded in secrecy and intrigue.

Inside a dimly lit warehouse, he exchanged hushed words with several individuals before handing me a small wooden box. "There are water and dry provisions inside," he explained.

"You'll be placed in a larger crate," he added, pointing to a nearby wooden box marked with "Fragile. Handle with care." and upward arrows indicating it shouldn't be overturned.

Though the roughly constructed crate had gaps for ventilation, making suffocation unlikely, the thought of being confined in such a cramped space filled me with dread. Shaking my head, I asked, "Is there no other way?"

The guy spread his hands in resignation. "No, but you don't have to endure too much discomfort. Once on the ship, you can use tools to pry open the wooden box at night and slip out. If you have enough money, you could even become the captain's VIP. But be cautious before you board."

"When will this batch of goods be loaded onto the ship?" I pressed.

"Tonight," he replied. "You need to get into the box now. I wish you success."

I had more questions, but the guy left impatiently. Several workers approached, guiding me to a wooden box and motioning for me to get inside.

I had no other choice. As I climbed into the box, the men immediately added the lid, "bang bang," nailing it shut. I felt a shiver of dread; it was as if I were lying in a coffin, with someone sealing the lid.

CHAPTER 4

Long Journey

I believe that, although there are many people in the world, only a handful have experienced what I am now enduring.

Hugging my knees, I sat down, placing the tools and food in front of me. There was actually enough space in the box to stretch my hands. Since it was still early, I decided to take a rest.

Unexpectedly, I fell asleep. When I woke up, a rumbling sound filled the air. Through the gaps between the boards, I saw a crane lifting a large wooden box. There were hundreds of boxes like mine, all being hoisted onto a large truck. Once the truck was loaded, it drove off.

I was almost on the ship. I thought that after boarding, I could explore a bit. As long as the ship set sail, it wouldn't matter if I was discovered.

Feeling optimistic, I waited for about an hour before my box was finally hoisted up. As it swayed in the air, I looked down through the cracks and saw the dock bustling with police on high alert. I secretly rejoiced; so far, everything had gone smoothly.

Once inside the cabin, I sensed something was wrong. Almost immediately, I heard a "bang" as another box was placed on top of mine. I nearly screamed in frustration—didn't the 19th Level have any arrangement to put my box on the outside?

Of course, I didn't dare to scream. I could only anxiously hope that, despite the box above me, there would be no one nearby.

Half an hour later, my hopes were dashed. There were wooden boxes all around me; my hiding place was among hundreds of crates! That meant I would have no chance to escape the box during the long journey.

How could this be? How was it possible? My mind raced with the dilemma: Should I shout loudly?

If I shouted, I might escape, but I would undoubtedly fall into the hands of the police. If I didn't, could I survive the 20-day sea voyage in this wooden box? The thought was unimaginable!

Finally, I shouted, realizing that being buried alive for a month was too terrifying to endure. I'd rather be discovered and captured.

I screamed as loud as I could, but after five minutes, it dawned on me that it was too late. The large wooden boxes surrounding me must have muffled my voice, and even if it could be heard, it would be faint. The crane's noise must have drowned out my cries, and no one heard me.

I could only hear the continuous sound of boxes being stacked around me. Large wooden boxes piled up above and around my hiding place.

Frustration turned to desperation as I took out a special nail-prying tool. I easily pried open the wooden box, but I couldn't get out—another box blocked my path.

I pushed the box with all my might, hoping to topple it and draw attention to my plight. But no matter how hard I tried, I couldn't move it.

Turning on my flashlight, I cautiously shone it on the wooden box in front of me.

Desperation fueled my determination as I meticulously pried open the wooden box. My hands felt the bundles inside—cotton fabrics. I was surrounded by millions of packages filled with these cotton fabrics, each box packed tightly.

With limited space to move, I painstakingly stuffed the cotton fabrics from the box in front of me into my own hiding box. The effort left me exhausted, but at last, I managed to open a small gap.

As I paused to catch my breath, a sense of relief washed over me. I realized I could use this same method to move forward slowly and create a "tunnel."

By prying open the box ahead, removing its contents, and advancing step by step, I could carve out an escape route. It was like navigating a life-sized maze, requiring immense effort to gain even a small distance.

Even if there were ten layers of wooden boxes before me, I knew I could get out after ten attempts. The realization invigorated me. If I could maintain this pace, I could escape in twenty hours, and there weren't even ten layers of boxes!

Excited, I sprang into action, starting to "dig" my tunnel. It was a unique tunnel carved through stacks of cotton fabric boxes. I managed to navigate through three wooden boxes, then took a break, ate some dry food, and continued my work.

After prying open the sixth wooden box, I couldn't help but cheer—there were no more wooden boxes blocking my way! But as I shone my flashlight forward, I gasped.

My tunnel had succeeded, but other goods were piled outside the cotton fabrics. In front of me was a massive coil of wire. I was stumped—how could I deal with the wire? Unless I had a sword capable of cutting through iron, I had no way to move it.

Unfortunately, such a sword was only a fantasy. Reality demanded a more practical solution.

I wouldn't be foolish enough to try moving the coils of wire, each weighing about a ton, with hundreds piled in front of me.

Feeling defeated, I sat down. The continuous effort of over ten hours left my bones aching, and the realization that my struggles had been in vain only added to my exhaustion.

I collapsed into the wooden box like a dead man, losing track of time. The ship seemed to be moving, and there were no regular machine sounds around me. I knew I was trapped in the cargo hold as the ship set sail.

I didn't want to move. I sat there, motionless, and in my extreme fatigue, I slowly drifted into sleep.

When I woke up, I checked my watch. It had not stopped, and I realized I had slept for over ten hours. My entire body was sore. I instinctively tried to straighten up, forgetting I was confined in the box. As soon as I pushed my body upwards, my head collided with the box with a loud "bang."

The pain snapped me back to clarity. I realized I wasn't entirely desperate—my "tunnel" had been blocked by the wire, but it didn't have to go straight forward. I could make the tunnel turn upwards!

Typically, cargo in the hold doesn't reach the top of the cabin, leaving a gap. If I could break through the top wooden box, I'd have a chance to climb out, over the wire or other goods, and escape.

I started working again, finding the task easier this time. As soon as I broke the boxes, the cotton fabrics inside would fall automatically, saving me effort.

After breaking through six more boxes, I finally climbed to the top of a pile of wooden crates. There was more space than I expected, allowing me to stand up straight.

I turned on my flashlight and cautiously walked over the wire. Beyond it were sacks of goods. I was "buried" in the corner of the cargo hold. It dawned on me that this situation wasn't due to negligence from the 19th-Level. It must have been deliberately arranged — he didn't want to kill me, but he certainly wanted me to suffer.

I am not one to let go of a grudge. As I climbed down past the sacks, my resolve hardened: I would find a way to make the 19th-Level experience the suffocating dread of being buried alive.

After navigating the sacks, I found myself in the narrow gaps of the cargo hold. Quickly, I spotted an iron ladder leading upwards. Typically, the cargo hold is locked when the ship is sailing, but it's checked regularly.

Initially, I planned to wait for someone to come down for an inspection, but my desire for fresh air changed my mind.

Eager for a breath of freedom, I climbed up the iron ladder and reached the hatch cover. With a hard push, I managed to create a crack. Using a very sharp thin saw blade—one of my many small tools—I reached through the crack and sawed. Fortunately, the cargo ship was old and dilapidated, allowing me to break the lock and escape the cabin.

The moment I pushed open the hatch and breathed in fresh air, the joy and relief were indescribable. It was midnight, shrouded in darkness.

Climbing onto the deck, I took several deep breaths, savoring the freedom. I walked forward ten steps and nestled into a lifeboat hanging beside the ship's side, a perfect hiding spot. It was well-concealed, unlikely to be discovered even during daylight, let alone at night.

With a clear mind, I began to strategize my next move.

Had I not caused chaos in the cargo hold, I could have revealed myself and approached the captain. With the captain's supreme authority at sea, my request might have appealed to his sense of power. However, I had ruined twelve large wooden boxes, turning their cotton fabrics into a mess. Admitting this to the captain would surely result in my immediate detention.

I had to devise another way to survive this long voyage.

Securing water was my priority. Food was manageable, thanks to my stash of dry provisions. The most reliable source of water would be the kitchen.

After some thought, I decided to head towards the stern. As I moved forward, I heard footsteps and conversation approaching. Quickly, I slipped into a dark corner.

Two sailors walked by, seemingly on duty, carrying long flashlights. However, they hadn't switched them on and didn't notice me.

As they walked and talked, I overheard their conversation.

"Do you think the man and woman in the captain's room are a bit strange?" one sailor asked.

"Of course," the other replied. "They hide whenever they see people. It must be that the captain took money to protect them smuggling out of the country. Damn, being a captain has such perks. We have to take risks when we smuggle goods!"

The first one laughed. "Of course it's good to be a captain. I think this man and woman must be very important. Otherwise, why would the captain order that no one but the waiters can enter his room?"

The other sailor muttered a few more curses, and they gradually walked away.

Hearing their conversation sparked a flurry of doubts in my mind. Two mysterious guests in the captain's room—a man and a woman. Could they be Brian and Luna? The mere thought of it made my blood boil.

If it was them, why had the 19th-Level operative arranged for their comfort in the captain's room while I suffered in the cargo hold? The injustice ignited a fire within me.

Determined to uncover the truth, I devised a new plan. The captain was openly accepting bribes to smuggle people out of the country, and I had leverage. If exposed, he would face severe punishment from the maritime court. This meant that even if I had destroyed twelve boxes of cotton fabrics, he would be powerless against me.

With newfound resolve, I emerged from the shadows and shouted, "Hey, stop for a moment!"

The two sailors, startled by the unexpected call, quickly turned around. As I strode confidently toward them, their expressions turned to shock.

"Who... who are you?" one of them stammered.

In a deep, commanding voice, I replied, "Don't bother with who I am. Just take me to see the captain!"

The two sailors exchanged uneasy glances before one of them spoke, "We can't do that. We need to inform the boatswain, who will report to the second mate, who will then report to the first mate, and finally, the captain."

I laughed, pulling out two large bills and handing one to each sailor. "No need to take me to the captain. Just show me where his room is."

Overjoyed, the sailors pointed to the top of the stairs. "Go up from here. The first door is the dining room for senior crew members; the second door is the captain's room."

I waved at the two sailors and dashed forward, heading straight for the staircase. I quickly climbed up, reaching the area reserved for the ship's senior crew. It was strictly off-limits to ordinary sailors unless summoned by the captain—stepping onto those stairs without permission was against the rules.

Halfway up the ladder, a sharp voice barked from above, "Who goes there? Halt!"

Ignoring the command, I quickened my pace. The voice shouted again, and I heard the sound of a bolt being drawn. But there was no time to shoot—I lunged forward and delivered a swift strike to the person's arm, causing the gun to fall.

With a deft move, I hooked the gun with my foot, sending it flying into my hand.

The young man, likely a fresh navigation school trainee, staggered back, stunned. "What... what is this for? Are you... are you going to rebel? Put down the gun!"

I coldly replied, "You're mistaken. I am not a sailor."

His eyes widened in shock. "So, who... who are you?"

Sneering, I retorted, "You want to know who I am? Why don't you ask about the man and woman in the captain's room?"

His face turned pale with embarrassment. "How... how did you know?"

Lowering my voice, I aimed the gun at him. "Take me to see them!"

The man was shocked. "The captain has ordered that no one is allowed to see them."

I laughed at his unwavering loyalty to the captain's orders. "Now I order you to take me to them."

Glancing at the gun, he hesitantly turned and led the way.

We reached the second door. The man raised his hand and knocked.

Less than a minute later, a voice came from inside: "Who is it? We're already asleep."

It was Brian Xi's voice! I recognized it immediately.

I pointed my gun at the man's waist, and he quickly responded, "It's me, it's me. The captain has a message for you. Please open the door and let me in."

I whispered in his ear, "You're doing well."

He gave me a bitter smile, and the door slowly creaked open.

The moment it did, I pushed the man aside and charged forward, shoulder first, bursting through the door with a loud "bang." Brian Xi's voice rang out in anger, "What's going on?"

I spun around and kicked the door shut, aiming my pistol at him.

The dim light in the cabin was enough for him to recognize me. Behind Brian Xi stood Luna. The captain's bedroom was quite luxurious, and both of them wore opulent pajamas. The captain must have received substantial benefits to surrender his quarters to them.

I stared at them, and they stared back. Their expressions, frozen in utter disbelief, were comical.

My unexpected appearance was beyond their wildest nightmares.

The joy in my heart was indescribable.

I tossed the gun in my hand and took two steps forward, settling onto a sofa. Raising the gun, I commanded, "Please sit down. Make yourselves comfortable."

Brian Xi remained standing in shock, but his wife regained her composure, managing a strained smile. "Mr. Morris, you're on a ship now," she said.

I was momentarily puzzled by her remark—of course, I knew I was on a ship.

I merely sneered, saying nothing.

She continued, "On this ship, the captain has supreme authority, and we can assure you that he's entirely on our side."

I couldn't help but laugh. "Haha!" It was clear she was trying to intimidate me. Did she really think a few words could scare me away? It was absurdly funny.

Laughing loudly, I said, "The captain may very well end up on trial, just like you. If that's 'on your side,' then sure."

At that moment, I heard movement outside the door. My voice must have alarmed the captain. I shouted, "Get out of here if you don't want to be sentenced to life imprisonment!"

The sounds outside ceased abruptly. Mrs. Xi's face turned ashen; she finally grasped that, on this ship, I held the supreme authority, not the captain.

I waved the gun again and said, "Sit down. Let's talk this through. The voyage is long, and we need a better resolution. If you two disappear, the captain would be thrilled—the evidence of his crimes would vanish."

Brian Xi finally spoke, urging, "Let's sit down first. Don't be afraid. Don't be afraid."

I smiled. "You're right. The situation is dire for you, but it's nothing compared to waiting on death row."

Brian Xi forced a bitter smile. "Mr. Morris, please forgive me. I didn't mean to betray you."

I narrowed my eyes. "Really?"

Brian Xi said, "Really, you know, I escaped from death row, and of course, I wanted to evade the police immediately. I didn't want to wait any longer, so I drove away. Later, when I tried to contact you again, it was impossible."

His explanation seemed reasonable.

However, having been fooled by him once, I wasn't about to be deceived again. I replied, "Really? It seems you're very honest."

Brian Xi and his wife exchanged glances. Mrs. Xi asked, "So, Mr. Morris, what are you going to do now?"

I said, "You know what I want. I want to know why you killed your brother!" I pointed directly at Brian Xi.

Before he could respond, Mrs. Xi screamed, "He didn't kill his brother."

I coldly retorted, "I'm asking him, not you!"

Under my gaze, Brian Xi lowered his head and remained silent. This was his "standard demeanor" after the incident, the same posture he adopted after pushing his brother off the cliff. He kept his head down, saying nothing, to deal with any interrogation.

Photos of him in this posture were published in almost every newspaper, and I had seen them many times.

I sneered, "You won't say it?"

Brian Xi still didn't respond.

I stood up and said, "I'll go see the captain. I want him to turn the ship around immediately. I think he will agree. And Mr. Xi, legally speaking, you should have been executed long ago. As soon as you get ashore, you'll be sent straight to the electric chair!"

Brian Xi remained silent.

To my surprise, Mrs. Xi suddenly got angry. She turned to Brian Xi, shouting, "You should speak up. Why don't you speak up? I'm sure you didn't kill anyone. Why don't you defend yourself? Why? You should speak up!"

I interjected, "Mrs. Xi, don't you know the inside story?"

Mrs. Xi shook her head angrily. "I don't know anything. I only know that he has a good heart and is definitely not someone who would kill. This, I am sure of!"

"But many people saw him push someone off the cliff!"

"Yes, I believe it, but why? Brian, tell me, why?"

Brian Xi finally spoke. He spread his hands and, with a faint smile, said in a weak voice, "I... had to do it. I had to."

As soon as he spoke, my questions came out like a barrage. "Why did you have to kill him? You went through so much effort to find him, and in the few days after he returned, you never quarreled. Why did you kill him?"

Brian Xi opened his mouth wide and, after a long pause, said, "It's useless. Even if I tell you, you won't... believe it."

I leaned in, almost touching his nose. "Talk. Just talk. I can believe anything, as long as it's the truth!"

Brian Xi looked at me for a long time. I thought he was about to speak, but he shook his head, sighed, and lowered his head again.

At that moment, something unexpected happened. Mrs. Xi, who had seemed so virtuous and quiet, suddenly lunged forward and slapped Brian Xi across the face without hesitation.

The sharp sound of the slap shocked me. Before I could react, Mrs. Xi scolded him, "Speak, you useless man! I want you to speak immediately!"

I had already noted that Mrs. Xi was a strong and capable woman, while Brian Xi was a cowardly man. This was the crux of the problem: why would a good person with a cowardly character push his brother off a cliff?

Now, I could clearly see that Mrs. Xi was trying to provoke Brian Xi into being strong and telling the truth. This was no act for my benefit. It showed that even Mrs. Xi didn't know why Brian Xi had killed.

After the slap, Brian Xi's face turned an ugly mix of blue and white, his body trembling. He covered his face with his hands but still said nothing.

I realized that the hardest thing in the world is to extract a secret from someone who refuses to speak. As long as they remain silent, there's nothing you can do.

Brian Xi's body shook for a full five minutes before he almost cried out, "Okay, if you force me to say it, I will say it, I will say it——"

He repeated "I will say it" twice but still didn't reveal the truth. I clenched my fists in frustration, fearing he might change his mind and render all my efforts futile.

He paused for what felt like an eternity, half a minute that was truly unbearable.

Finally, Brian Xi spoke. "I pushed him down because he... he can no longer be considered a human being!"

I was stunned. I didn't understand what he meant. I glanced at Mrs. Xi, whose face was also full of surprise. She clearly didn't understand either.

I looked back at Brian Xi, needing clarification. But seeing his state, I held back.

He was trembling so violently that his teeth chattered, making a "de de" sound. His expression was so agitated that I couldn't bear to press him further.

He shook for a long time before grabbing the headboard tightly, which seemed to calm him.

Gasping, he said, "Do you understand? I really had to push him down."

I couldn't help but smile bitterly. I was confused by his words. I tried to speak calmly, "I don't understand. He is obviously a human. How can you say he is not a human?"

Brian Xi suddenly raised his voice and screamed, "He is not a human! He is not a human! People die. He will not die. What is this?"

After his outburst, he stared at me, waiting for an answer.

But I had none. I could only stare back.

I didn't know what Brian Xi meant. How could I answer? He claimed that Mark wouldn't die. People always die. By that logic, those who don't die can't be considered human. However, if Mark was a "person" who wouldn't die, then Brian Xi's crime of murder wouldn't stand. After all, how could he be guilty of "killing" someone who wouldn't die?

CHAPTER 5

Failure

My mind was in turmoil, overwhelmed with so many thoughts that I didn't know where to begin. At this moment, I heard Mrs. Xi say, "Darling, please explain more clearly. You didn't kill him, right?"

"I... killed him!"

"But you just said that he wouldn't die."

"I pushed him off such a high cliff. I think... I think he is probably dead. I... really don't know."

"Tell me slowly. First, explain why he wouldn't die."

"He... took a medicine."

"A medicine? What medicine?"

"The medicine for immortality."

"The medicine for immortality?"

At this point, I couldn't contain myself. I shouted, "Stop talking! What's the point of saying such meaningless words?"

Mrs. Xi turned to me, her eyes almost reproachful. "Mr. Morris, can't you hear that what he's saying is the key to the whole incident?"

I sneered, "What is the key?"

"The elixir of immortality," she replied.

I waved my hand dismissively, showing my disgust. "Do you think Mark has obtained something that even the ancient emperor couldn't acquire?"

My question dripped with sarcasm. Yet, Mrs. Xi's response was sharp and cutting. "We now have many things that even the ancient emperor couldn't have dreamed of, don't we?"

I rolled my eyes. She had a point, and I was left speechless for a moment.

Mrs. Xi continued, "So, this is not meaningless. Mr. Morris, as his wife, I can tell that what he's saying now is a crucial truth."

I had no rebuttal. "Okay, go on then."

I gestured at Brian. Before I could finish, he said, "I've said all I want to say."

Mrs. Xi quickly interjected, "No, there's more. Even if he took a kind of medicine, the so-called elixir of immortality, why did you push him off the cliff?"

Brian trembled, covering his face with his hands. After a moment, he admitted, "He wants me to take this immortality medicine too."

"Does he have this medicine with him?" she asked.

"No, he wants me to go to a deserted island where he found it after getting lost at sea during the war," Brian replied.

Things began to make sense. Mark disappeared during a military operation, drifting to a small, unnoticed island. There, he found and took the immortality medicine until Brian discovered him.

The relationship between the brothers was evidently strong, as Mark wanted his brother to take the immortality medicine too. But if Brian didn't want to live forever, why did he push Mark off the cliff?

"Did you refuse?" I asked.

Brian remained silent, not even nodding or shaking his head. Mrs. Xi tried asking a few questions, but he said nothing.

Mrs. Xi sighed and turned to me. "Mr. Morris, can you let him calm down first? We can't run away on the ship. Let him rest, and we'll ask him again tomorrow, okay?"

I agreed. Brian was clearly too agitated to continue. Besides, with a nearly month-long voyage ahead, we had time.

"Mr. Xi, calm down first. See you tomorrow," I said, retreating to the door and closing it behind me.

Turning around, I found a middle-aged man standing there, his face pale and lips quivering. From his attire, I recognized him as the captain.

"Captain, you sure know how to make money!" I sneered.

The captain almost cried, "Who are you...? Let's discuss..."

I cut him off. "Discuss what? Whether I accepted bribes?"

I didn't reveal my identity, but my words strongly implied that I was someone with the authority to accept bribes.

The captain smiled bitterly. "Yes... yes."

I nodded. "Then it depends on your sincerity."

"I am sincere," he hurriedly assured me.

"Fine. First, find me a place to eat and sleep. Preferably your current quarters," I demanded.

"Okay, okay," the captain agreed.

"Then, we'll discuss further," I concluded.

The captain smiled bitterly. "Sir, I think you are not going to report me, right?"

I smiled and said, "It seems so, but it depends on whether I am comfortable here. Do you understand?"

The captain nodded repeatedly and let me into his bedroom.

His bedroom was just as luxurious as I had imagined. I fell onto the bed without hesitation, while he stood awkwardly aside.

Waving my hand dismissively, I said, "Go and arrange a place to sleep for yourself. I'll be borrowing this place temporarily."

The captain immediately agreed and walked out.

Lying on the bed, I felt a wave of comfort wash over me. Treating this corrupt captain like this and finding Brian and his wife had filled me with satisfaction. I couldn't help but whistle as I drifted off to sleep.

I was awakened by a loud "bang."

Opening my eyes, I thought I was dreaming. I couldn't understand what had happened. The captain, who had been so respectful before, now stood at the door in a neat uniform, holding a pistol with a fierce look.

With a wave of his arm, four or five tall crew members rushed towards me.

It was clear that these men meant me harm. I naturally knew this, but I couldn't fathom why the captain had suddenly turned against me. Was he always afraid I would leak his secrets and now wanted to kill me?

If that were the case, he should have killed me while I was asleep, instead of openly sending strong men to deal with me. But other than this, what else can he rely on?

As I pondered this, the crew members reached my bed.

The captain pointed his gun at me and shouted, "Catch him!"

I stretched out my hand. "Don't move! Captain, don't you think about yourself when you do this?"

The captain grinned. "You are a wanted fugitive who sneaked onto my ship. I will keep you here and hand you over to the police when we return!"

I sneered. "Are you going to detain me alone, or the other two?"

By "the other two," I meant Brian and his wife. My words were a reminder to the captain that I still had leverage over him.

Unexpectedly, the captain laughed. "Shut up!" he roared, clearly fearless.

I quickly assessed the situation. He had a gun, and there were four or five men in front of me. However, his intention to arrest me suggested he didn't dare to kill me, giving me a chance to act.

Spreading my hands, I said, "Shut up and—"

I bent my body and suddenly jumped up from the bed. The bed's elasticity made my leap fast and powerful.

As I jumped, I attacked with both hands and feet, hitting three men simultaneously.

They howled and fell back, while I rolled to the captain's feet.

The captain didn't realize I was at his feet until it was too late.

I grabbed his legs and dragged him down, slashing his wrist to snatch the pistol. Jumping up, I slammed the hatch shut, stood with my back against the door, and shouted, "Stand up, put your hands on your heads!"

The crew members, seeing the gun in my hand, had no choice but to comply.

The captain lay on the ground for a long time before standing up. Touching the back of his head, he glared at me. "You can't escape legal punishment."

"Maybe," I replied. "We may be locked up in the same cell."

"Why should I go to jail?" he shouted.

"Your memory is too bad. In the room opposite, you smuggled two wanted criminals out of the country. One of them has been sentenced to death. Have you forgotten?"

The captain took a breath. "You can't threaten me."

"What do you mean?" I asked, stunned.

"They are gone."

"Gone?" I almost couldn't believe my ears.

The captain, though embarrassed, wore a proud expression. "Gone. They put down the lifeboat and left secretly. You have no evidence!"

I was truly stunned.

The news hit me like a ton of bricks! It wasn't just because I could no longer threaten the captain—he wasn't my target.

The real blow came from the dire situation I found myself in after they left.

Originally, I had two ways to change my circumstances: One was to prove Brian was not guilty. The second was to take him back to prison.

Without Brian, both options vanished, leaving me eternally wanted!

For a full minute, I was stunned before I finally spoke. "This is impossible. We're at sea. What are their chances of survival after getting off a lifeboat? Why would they take this risk?"

The captain said, "How should I know?"

I said sternly, "You're hiding them both!"

The captain laughed calmly. "If you think so, after we arrive at port, you can accuse me to the local police. But when they can't find anyone, you'll be in trouble."

In the captain's calm, smug look, I saw that Brian and his wife really had left!

They chose to drift on the vast ocean, clearly trying to escape me. While they were making their getaway, I was sound asleep. I felt like bashing my head with the butt of my gun—how could I have been so foolish to think they wouldn't leave while we were still on the ship!

Their departure left me in an indescribable predicament.

Honestly, I had no idea what to do next.

The captain smirked darkly at me, "Put down your gun. If you really want to leave, I can provide you with a lifeboat, water, and food."

Conflicted, I realized there was no point in staying on the ship without them. But what was the point of drifting at sea?

The ocean is vast. Could two lifeboats possibly meet?

In my life, I've never faced consecutive failures like now.

My opponents weren't even formidable: just a death row prisoner and a woman.

After a long while, I calmed down. "Captain, send these people out. I need to talk to you alone."

The captain said coldly, "Give me the gun first."

I hesitated. Without the gun, he'd control me. But even with it, what did I control now?

I had failed, completely.

The captain stretched out his hand, grinning. "Give it to me!"

"Captain, I'm a real desperado now. You should understand that a true desperado dares to do anything!" I said.

The captain's face changed, his voice a bit shaky. "But your current crime doesn't warrant death!"

Finally, a small turn. He feared I would shoot him. Naturally, I wouldn't let go of the gun. "For me, it's almost the same," I said.

His face paled further.

"Of course, if you don't push me too hard, I won't do anything," I added.

The captain gave in slightly. "So, what do you want?"

I was at a loss, unsure how to answer. All this failure had nearly sapped my will to start over. Without that determination, I didn't know what to do.

He asked again, "What do you want?"

I had to give him a ridiculous answer. "Please wait. Let me think."

The captain looked at me, astonished. My mind was in a mess, but I quickly thought through my options.

What should I do?

The ideal situation would involve a helicopter and a speedboat to search for Brian and his wife. But on this dilapidated cargo ship, there were no such luxuries.

Should I also drift in a lifeboat?

If I did, my chances of finding them were zero.

I certainly shouldn't be that foolish. So what could I do?

The captain urged me again.

I asked, "Can this cargo ship stop somewhere nearby?"

The captain quickly shook his head. "Absolutely not. We must sail directly to Timor Island on schedule."

"What if we encounter danger on the way?" I asked coldly.

The captain also replied to me honestly and bluntly: "If we encounter danger on the way, it will be different, because this will prevent the ship from reaching its destination forever. This ship is too old and cannot be in danger."

I sighed, realizing I had no other choice but to take a gamble. I was certain that Brian and his wife hadn't abandoned me and taken the lifeboat to drift aimlessly at sea without a plan. They must have had a purpose—perhaps they even carried distress signaling equipment. If that were the case, their chances of being rescued were quite high.

Since they had chosen a cargo ship bound for Timor Island, it was likely that, once rescued, they would still head there. I could wait for them on that island.

Of course, all of this was just speculation. If even one of my assumptions turned out to be wrong, I might never see them again.

When I said I had to gamble, I meant that, under these circumstances, I had no choice but to treat my assumptions as facts and act accordingly.

I said to the captain: "Then, my request is very simple. I want to live on the ship and have good treatment. When the ship reaches the destination, you must cover me to go ashore."

The captain thought for a while: "Do you promise not to implicate me?" I said: "Of course, what else can I do to implicate you?"

The captain nodded: "Then, don't make trouble on the ship, and it's best not to contact the sailors."

I put away the pistol and said: "I can do it. I hope you don't play tricks, because when you get off the ship, I will threaten you with a gun and won't give you a chance to harm me."

After I finished speaking, I retreated to the room occupied by Brian and his wife and fell on the bed.

I felt a splitting headache, and I had to hug my head tightly to feel a little better.

The next twenty days of the voyage can be said to be the most boring time in my life. I borrowed a radio and listened to the news every day, hoping to get some news about Brian. Because if the two of them were discovered and their identities were known, it would definitely be big news that shook the world. However, I didn't get any news. I was almost bored in this cabin every day.

The ship finally arrived at its destination!

I was certain that if I had arrived a few days later, the sheer monotony of those endless days would have driven me mad. After completing the port entry formalities, the captain and I disembarked together.

The captain was well-acquainted with Timor Island, and the Portuguese officials knew him personally. Aware that my only intention was to leave and not to harm him, the captain remained remarkably composed.

Once he led me to the Chinese community and I was convinced he meant me no harm, I finally returned his pistol. He turned and left swiftly, while I stepped into a Chinese restaurant.

The waiters, all Chinese, showed keen interest when I mentioned I had some US dollars to exchange for local currency, even at a slight loss. After exchanging a decent amount, I endured a meal that I could have cooked better with my eyes closed—a so-called "Chinese dish." I then checked into a mid-range hotel at the end of the street.

Now that I was on Timor Island, it was time to get to work. I quickly befriended a dozen or so idle teenagers loitering on the streets. Offering them a modest reward, I tasked them with finding a Chinese couple. I described Brian and his wife in detail and instructed them to keep a constant watch on the docks for any Chinese arrivals.

My operation expanded rapidly. Within three days, I had 146 street kids working for me, yet I hadn't received any useful information.

I sent another telegram to Mr. Miller, informing him of my arrival in Timor and requesting a transfer of funds for expenses. The money arrived at the local bank the very next day.

I spent my days combing the island for any trace of Brian and his wife.

Timor was a peculiar place—a strange blend of old and new, where paradise and hell coexisted. As a Portuguese colony, it served as a penal settlement for criminals from Portugal and its other territories, yet it also had its own pockets of prosperity and beauty.

Sitting on the beach, gazing at the South Pacific as the waves rolled in, carrying pristine seashells to my feet, felt no different from lounging in a Hawaiian bay.

But after two weeks of waiting, I was on the verge of losing hope.

Then, one evening, as I sat on the beach as usual, two of the street kids came running toward me, breathless and shouting, "Sir, sir! We think we've earned that reward!"

I had promised a hefty sum to anyone who could locate Brian and his wife, so their words immediately sparked my excitement.

"You found them? Where?" I asked urgently.

"On Mr. Mr. Poggin's yacht!" they exclaimed in unison.

Although I hadn't been on Timor Island long—just about two weeks—I had learned of Mr. Poggin by my second day there.

He was one of the most powerful and wealthy men on the island, so when the two boys mentioned him, I was taken aback. "Are you sure you didn't mistake them for someone else?" I asked.

They eagerly replied, "No mistake! We even know how they got here!"

I pressed, "How did they come?"

The boys beamed with pride. "People at the dock said they were drifting at sea and rescued by a ship. They sent a telegram to Mr. Poggin from the ship, and he personally went out on his yacht to bring them back. So, sir, do we get the reward?"

I had already pulled out the money. "Of course."

I handed the cash to them, and they were overjoyed. They added, "When we left, Mr. Poggin's yacht had just docked. They're probably at his house now. Do you know where his 'Paradise Garden' is?"

Mr. Poggin's estate was famously known as "Paradise Garden" because it housed ten rare birds of paradise—a fact everyone on the island knew.

CHAPTER 6

A Bunch of Idiots

Moreover, almost everyone on the island knew exactly where Paradise Garden was located.

I sprang into action, leaving the beach behind. The two boys trailed after me, and I said, "I know where Paradise Garden is. But I need your help—keep this quiet, don't spread the word."

The boys ran off, shouting, "Got it!"

I headed straight to the marina where the yachts were docked. There, I spotted the Paradise, a large ocean-going yacht. A few crew members were on deck, scrubbing away. It was clear the owner wasn't onboard.

I didn't linger long at the marina and soon made my way to Paradise Garden.

The journey from the marina to the estate was quite a distance, but I wasn't in a hurry. I strolled along, whistling casually, feeling completely at ease.

After all, Xi and his wife would never expect me to still be on the island, waiting for them. I could already picture the look of sheer shock on their faces when I showed up again.

I silently vowed to myself that this time, no matter what, I wouldn't fall for their tricks again.

By the time I reached Paradise Garden, darkness had fully settled.

A formal meeting was out of the question; the guards at the entrance would undoubtedly turn me away. Instead, I seized a moment of their inattention, dashed under the wall, and slipped into the shadows.

Then, using a thin, tough rope with a hook at one end, I scaled the wall swiftly. But as I neared the top, I froze.

Circles of wire mesh crowned the wall, and the hook was now touching the mesh, creating a "sizzling" sound and sparking. The wire mesh was clearly electrified.

I hesitated. My body couldn't touch the electric wire. My only option was to leap forward and clear the electrified mesh.

The wire wasn't very high, so jumping over it wasn't the issue. The real question was: could I land safely on the other side? To find out, I needed to first determine if there were any traps waiting for me inside the fence.

I climbed up a little, trying to stretch my head forward without touching the wire mesh. I bent my body and stepped on the top of the wall with the toes of my feet, but it was too dark to see the situation at the foot of the wall.

In that moment, I had to take a risk. I gathered my strength and suddenly bounced up, turning a hollow somersault in mid-air.

My body fell rapidly, and just as I thought I was about to land, I straightened myself.

Suddenly, with a "whoosh," a long black shadow rushed towards me in the darkness!

Even in the darkness, I could tell it was a highly trained wolfhound.

The dog lunged at me so suddenly that, under normal circumstances, I would have had no chance to react. But in this case, I had to thank its trainer. The dog had been trained too well—it didn't bark, and instead of going for my legs or arms, it went straight for my throat.

If it had aimed for my legs, I would have been helpless. But targeting my throat gave me a slim chance. Protecting my throat with my hands was far easier. As I had jumped down, I'd kept hold of the rope with the hook attached.

In a split second, I swung my right hand, driving the hook hard into the dog's upper jaw. The force was so strong that the steel hook nearly pierced through.

The wolfhound's jaws clamped shut, and I followed up with a sharp blow from my left palm to the sensitive spot between its eyes and nose.

The impact was solid. With a loud thud, both the dog and I tumbled to the ground.

I rolled several times and sprang back to my feet.

The wolfhound also rolled but didn't get up. It twitched its legs once and lay still—dead.

Only then did the full weight of the danger I'd just faced hit me.

Cold sweat began to pour from my body. A gust of wind blew, and I couldn't help but shiver!

I ran forward about ten yards close to the wall and stood still with my back against it.

Inside the wall was an expansive garden, essentially a hillside meticulously landscaped with trees and lawns. About two hundred paces away stood a large white house, with lights glowing from several of its windows.

Brian and his wife were undoubtedly inside that house.

The place was massive, so it was unlikely every room was occupied. If I could just get inside, finding a hiding spot would be easy.

I waited for a moment, knowing that the wolfhound's death would eventually alert someone to my presence. But I had neither the tools nor the time to bury the dog.

Using the shadows of the trees as cover, I moved swiftly toward the house.

As I approached the house, I suddenly heard someone shouting in Japanese.

I turned around and froze.

At least seven wolfhounds were charging forward, led by a rather short man—clearly Japanese. I immediately suspected he was a former Japanese military dog trainer from World War II.

The seven dogs were heading straight for the dead wolfhound. I knew my presence would be discovered any moment.

With so many dogs on my trail, my scent would make it impossible to hide. My only chance to avoid immediate danger was to get inside the house.

I sprinted around the building, staying close to the walls, until I reached a window. I pushed it, and to my surprise, it opened easily. I quickly climbed inside.

The room was pitch dark, but I could make out that it was a large study. I opened the door and found myself in a hallway with a staircase at the end.

As I dashed toward the stairs, I heard the pack of wolfhounds erupt into frenzied barking. The noise was rapidly closing in.

I bolted up the stairs just as the Japanese man's shouts and the dogs' barks entered the study below.

At the same time, a loud voice from the second floor demanded, "What's going on?"

For a moment, I was truly trapped—pursued from behind and blocked ahead. Fortunately, I had already reached the top of the stairs, so I quickly opened a door and slipped inside.

I knew I couldn't stay in this room for long. The dogs would soon track me here. As soon as I entered, I began searching for an exit.

But as I groped around, I realized the room was engulfed in complete darkness—not a single glimmer of light. I immediately concluded there were no windows. What could I do now?

Should I retreat? Outside, the dogs and their handler were closing in. There was no escape that way. My only option was to find another way out within this room.

I lifted my heel, removed a small flashlight from my shoe, and turned it on. My intention was to search for a sealed window or some other exit.

But when the beam of light fell on a face, I froze.

Standing silently across from me was a person. The sudden realization that someone had been there all along, unmoving and soundless, sent a chill down my spine. For a moment, I was paralyzed, unsure of what to do.

However, the figure remained completely still, showing no reaction to the light shining directly on its face.

My panic subsided as I realized it wasn't a person—it was a statue.

Just as I began to relax, thinking it might be a statue, the figure moved.

Although the movement was slight—just a slow blink of the eyes—it was enough to confirm that this was indeed a person. After all, statues don't blink.

I took a step back, intending to lean against the door and figure out my next move.

But as I stepped back, the barking dogs reached the door, and it suddenly burst open. Behind me, a sharp voice commanded, "Don't move! Stay where you are!"

With the door open, light from the hallway flooded in, and I could finally see the entire room.

What I saw left me frozen—not because of the command, but because I was utterly stunned.

What kind of place was this?

This wasn't a room; it was a cage.

The space was large but windowless, enclosed by solid walls. The beam of my small flashlight had only illuminated one person, but in reality, there were four standing right in front of me. All of them were short, dark-skinned, and muscular, dressed only in loincloths—clearly natives from a South Pacific island.

If it had just been those four, I might have kept my composure. But the room was filled with at least a hundred such natives.

Some were squatting, others sitting or lying down. Some huddled together, while others curled up alone.

Yet, it wasn't the sheer number of people that horrified me. What sent a chill through my bones was the indescribable eeriness in their expressions.

Saying their "expressions were eerie" isn't entirely accurate. In fact, their faces were completely blank, devoid of any emotion. They simply stared wide-eyed, occasionally blinking, their bodies almost frozen in their original positions.

What was this? Who were these people? My mind flooded with questions. The scene before me was so bizarre that I barely noticed what was happening behind me—until I felt something cold and metallic press against my back. I stiffened and let out a low grunt.

Then, a voice from behind ordered, "Turn around."

I hesitated briefly, but I was certain it was a gun pressed against me. I had no choice but to comply, so I slowly turned around.

The man holding the gun took a step back. He was a burly figure, clearly not the main player here—just a hired hand.

Next, I saw the Japanese man, with seven or eight wolfhounds crouched obediently at his side. Then, my eyes fell on a large man in an ornate robe—presumably Mr.Poggin.

I had expected to see Xi and his wife, but they were nowhere in sight.

With a gun pointed at me and a pack of wolfhounds watching my every move, resistance was out of the question.

The large man scrutinized me for a moment before demanding, "Who are you?"

I shrugged. "I think you already know who I am."

He barked again, louder this time, "Who are you?"

I still avoided a direct answer: "Didn't Brian Xi tell you? Why bother asking?"

The man had a short temper. He charged at me, his fat hand raised to slap me across the face.

If I had let him hit me, it would have been laughable. Just as his hand was about to strike, I raised my arm to block it, then twisted my wrist, gripping his firmly.

His attempt to hit me was a huge mistake. By moving closer, his large frame blocked me from the gun pointed at my back. If the wolfhounds tried to attack, they'd risk injuring him too.

To secure my position further, I pulled him back a step, using his body to block the doorway. This made me even safer.

I tightened my grip on his wrist, and beads of sweat formed on his forehead.

I asked coldly, "Do you know who I am now?"

His arrogance vanished. "Yes, yes!"

I sneered, "Aren't you going to call off the dogs and the gunmen?"

The wolfhounds were barking ferociously, so I had to raise my voice to be heard.

Mr. Poggin's voice was hoarse: "Go, all of you!"

His body blocked my view, but I heard the Japanese man's commands as the barking gradually faded.

Then, a nervous voice asked, "Mr. Poggin, if we leave, who will protect you?"

He exploded, "Idiot! Can't you see I don't need protection right now? Get out!"

Of course, he still needed protection—it was just that the gunmen couldn't help him at the moment.

The gunman stammered, "Yes, yes!"

I added, "Wait. Leave one gun on the floor and kick it over."

Mr. Poggin quickly echoed, "Do as he says!"

A gun slid across the floor. I bent down to pick it up and released his wrist. As I let go, the color slowly returned to the pale-faced man's cheeks. He rubbed his wrist, now deep purple from my grip, and said, "You should leave before the island's military and police surround this place."

I shrugged. "Why should I leave? Let them come."

As I spoke, I pressed the gun against his belly. His composure wavered again, and he wiped sweat from his brow. "Alright, what do you want?"

"I want to see two people."

"Who?"

"Brian Xi and his wife."

"I don't know them!"

I said coldly, "If you don't want a hole in your stomach, stop wasting time. This evening, those two were on your yacht. Has your memory come back now?"

He reluctantly nodded. "But they're not here. They went to my other villa."

That was believable. If Xi and his wife were in this house, they would have come out to face me by now, knowing they couldn't avoid me.

I said, "Fine. Take me there."

Poggin growled, "You won't get away with this. You'll never get away."

I shot back, "You'd better start praying now that I do get away. Because if I don't, the first thing I'll do is put a bullet in your stomach."

Poggin trembled with rage. He must have deeply regretted slapping me earlier.

But regret was useless. Hadn't I also regretted saving Brian Xi from the death cell?

I commanded, "Turn around!"

Poggin turned, and I said, "Now take me to Brian Xi. You'll drive. If anything goes wrong while we're leaving this house or on the road, you'll be the first to suffer, Mr.Poggin."

He grunted and started walking.

I followed, but after just one step, something struck me. "Wait!"

Poggin's bulky frame stopped. I asked, "Who are those people in that room?"

Poggin's body stiffened, but he didn't answer.

I asked again, but he remained silent.

This only deepened my suspicion. I couldn't help glancing back. The people in the room seemed completely oblivious to everything happening around them. Most remained in their original positions, occasionally blinking. They looked like a group of idiots, and it made me sick.

I decided not to press further. At this point, I couldn't see how these people were connected to Brian or my mission. I simply said, "Fine, don't answer. You'll talk eventually. Now, let's go."

Poggin walked slowly, and I stayed close behind.

At the staircase, four gunmen stood in our way, but they quickly stepped aside. Poggin and I descended the stairs, left the house, and entered the garage.

I forced him into the driver's seat of a luxurious sedan and sat behind him, my gun pressed against the back of his head. "Stay calm. Don't crash the car into a rock."

He drove through the garden and out the iron gate.

As soon as we passed through the iron gate, I breathed a sigh of relief. Glancing back, I saw many people rushing around in the garden, but no one was following us.

Since no one was chasing us, it was unlikely they would alert the local police. They had all witnessed Mr. Poggin's precarious situation, and any rash move could cost them their leader.

The car wound its way along the mountain road, which was rough in places. Even though Poggin's car was a top-tier luxury vehicle, it still jolted occasionally.

Every time the car hit a particularly rough patch, the gun in my hand would bump against Poggin's skull, making him groan involuntarily.

Outside the window, the surroundings were pitch black, with only the silhouettes of mountains rising and falling in the distance. The area was eerily quiet.

The car seemed to be heading deeper into the mountains. Finally, a cluster of lights appeared in the distance.

I knew that, given the circumstances, Poggin valued his life too much to try anything tricky. Seeing the lights and the faint outline of a house ahead reinforced my confidence.

The car finally stopped in front of a large, oddly designed villa, isolated with no other buildings nearby.

Poggin honked the horn, and in the overwhelming silence, the sound was startling.

Two men appeared at the iron gate, exclaiming, "Good heavens, Mr. Poggin, it's you!"

They hurriedly opened the gate, and Poggin drove in, coming to a stop at the stone steps. At that moment, I heard a window upstairs open, followed by Brian Xi's voice: "Mr. Poggin, what's the matter? It's already so late at night."

Poggin took a deep breath. "There's trouble, Mr. Xi. Your problems have caught up with you."

I was startled and immediately whispered, "Don't talk nonsense."

Poggin paused, then added, "I've brought a friend to see you. Come down!"

Brian hesitated for a moment but quickly replied, "Alright!"

Poggin let go of the steering wheel. "Can I get out now?"

Suddenly, I had a strange feeling: since arriving here, Poggin no longer seemed afraid of me.

Why? What had changed?

I quickly glanced at the gun in my hand. It was loaded—I had checked it as soon as I picked it up. But since Poggin's attitude had shifted, I needed to be extra cautious.

I said, "I'll get out first, then you follow."

Poggin chuckled. "Fine, whatever you say."

I opened the car door and stepped out. At the same time, the lights on the ground floor of the villa came on, and someone opened the door. Poggin also emerged from the car, stepping out sideways.

I immediately moved closer, keeping the gun pointed at his back.

Poggin didn't turn around but called out, "Mr. Xi!"

The villa door opened, and Brian and his wife appeared in the doorway. Poggin gestured toward me with his thumb. "Do you see who's come to visit you?"

His tone was casual, as if I were an old friend he hadn't seen in years.

Brian, of course, immediately recognized who was standing behind Poggin.

He and his wife were momentarily stunned but then broke into smiles. "What a small world!"

Their reaction left me utterly bewildered.

Brian showed no trace of surprise upon seeing me—this was utterly bizarre!

Logically, I had the upper hand, yet I felt like I had no control over the situation. They showed no fear of me whatsoever. What was going on?

I frowned and said sternly, "Brian, this time, you won't escape."

Brian spread his hands. "Why would I need to escape? That's ridiculous."

In that moment, a strange thought flashed through my mind: What if the man standing before me wasn't Brian at all?

CHAPTER 7

The Trap from the Start

But if that man wasn't Brian Xu, then who was he?

And yet, if he was Brian, why did his demeanor differ so drastically from the man I knew?

I pressed the barrel of my gun into Poggin's back. "Move. Inside. We'll talk there."

Poggin shuffled forward, his movements casual, almost as if there wasn't a gun pointed at his spine. But Poggin was no brave man—I knew him to be a coward, trembling at the slightest hint of danger. His calmness now was unnerving.

Once inside the grand hall, both Poggin and Brian sat down on the sofa without waiting for my command. They looked at me, their eyes gleaming with amusement, as though I were some pitiful clown performing for their entertainment.

Only Luna remained composed, her expression neutral, devoid of laughter.

I was still grappling with the situation. I raised my gun, ready to speak, but Brian cut me off with a chuckle. "Put the gun down. We can talk like civilized men."

I glared at him. "With someone like you, I prefer to talk with a gun in hand."

Brian sighed, almost theatrically, then clapped his hands twice. A native servant emerged, carrying a tray. On it lay a pistol.

The audacity of it stunned me. Here I was, holding Brian at gunpoint, and he had the gall to summon a servant to bring him a weapon. Was he a fool, or was there something I was missing?

My patience snapped. I pulled the trigger. The gunshot echoed through the hall, and the tray flew out of the servant's hands, the pistol clattering to the floor.

Brian laughed again, unfazed. "Relax, Mr. Morris. You must understand—guns are useless here."

I sneered. "They seem fairly useful to me."

He stood, puffing out his chest. "Oh? Then shoot me. Go ahead. Shoot."

His brazen challenge ignited my fury. "You think I won't?"

"Not at all," he replied, his voice dripping with mockery. "I'm *hoping* you will."

I had no choice but to fire. I didn't need to kill him, but I had to wound him—otherwise, I'd lose control of the situation entirely. I raised my gun and pulled the trigger.

The bullet tore through Brian's shoulder, exiting cleanly on the other side. He staggered slightly, but his smile never wavered.

I stared at him, my confidence in my marksmanship clashing with the impossible scene before me. I had shot him. I knew I had. The bullet had pierced his shoulder, yet he stood there, unharmed, not a drop of blood in sight.

I took a sharp breath. Brian reached up, tore open the fabric around his shoulder, and revealed the wound—a deep, clean hole. But there was no blood. No pain. And as I watched, the hole began to close, new flesh knitting together at an unnatural speed. Within minutes, the wound was gone, leaving no trace.

He smiled at me. "You see? Guns are useless here. You should believe me now."

My eyes darted to Luna, then to Poggin. Brian—or whoever he was—spoke again. "Don't bother looking. Everyone here is the same. We've all taken the elixir of immortality, my friend. Immortality."

My heart lurched, not at the mention of the elixir, but at his words. I gasped, "You're not Poggin?"

He nodded calmly. "You should have realized that by now."

I felt the room spin. I turned to Luna, desperation in my voice. "Mrs. Xi!"

She met my gaze coldly. "This is a private matter. I don't owe you an explanation."

Defeated, I slumped onto the sofa. I had failed—again. And this time, the failure was more crushing than ever.

Poggin and Brian—no, not Brian Xi, but Mark Xi—laughed openly. I forced myself to sit up, my voice trembling but defiant. "Mark Xi, you murdered your own brother?"

My accusation only fueled their laughter. But in that moment, one truth became clear: the man I had broken out of the death row cell, the man the world believed to be Brian Xi, was not him at all. He was Mark Xi. The murder case wasn't about Brian Xi killing his brother—it was Mark Xi killing his older brother.

The man who had plunged off the cliff, whose body was never found, was the true Brian Xi—a good man who had spent nearly two decades searching the remote islands of the South Pacific, only to find a monster. A murderer.

But this revelation didn't bring clarity. Instead, it tangled the web of mysteries even further. Questions piled upon questions, each one darker and more convoluted than the last. The truth remained shrouded, and I was no closer to understanding it.

The room felt heavier, the air thicker. I was trapped—not just in this hall, but in a labyrinth of lies and secrets, with no light to guide me out.

My mind was a whirlwind of chaos, the questions swirling like a storm. The enigma before me could be distilled into three burning questions:

1. *Why would Mark kill his brother?* Brian Xi had no reason to murder his younger brother, but Mark Xi—fresh from his exile on that desolate island—what motive could he possibly have? What had driven him to such a heinous act?

2. *Why had Luna played along with the deception?* After the murder, everyone had assumed the victim was Mark Xi. While their physical resemblance might explain the confusion, how could Brian's own wife, Luna, not recognize her husband? She had clearly orchestrated this charade, but why? What was her role in all of this?

3. *What was the truth behind the "elixir of immortality"?* How could a gunshot wound heal instantaneously, without so much as a drop of blood? What unnatural force was at work here? What had they discovered—or unleashed?

Beneath these monumental questions lay a tangled web of smaller mysteries, each one more perplexing than the last. My thoughts were so jumbled that I could barely form a coherent sentence.

After a long silence, I finally blurted out something that even I found absurd: "Are you... an alien?"

Mark paused, then burst into laughter. "You're reaching too far! Of course, I'm human. But now that you've uncovered my secret, I'm afraid your time is up. There's no need for further questions."

His words sent a jolt of panic through me. I leapt to my feet, but Mark only chuckled darkly. "We are immortal. How do you plan to escape?"

I shouted, "That's impossible! No living thing is immortal!"

He smirked, his voice dripping with malice. "A pity you won't have the chance to prove yourself wrong. If you did, you'd find that the natives here—their bones, when tested for radioactivity—would reveal they're each over a thousand years old. And they'll keep living, indefinitely."

His words hung in the air, a chilling testament to the unimaginable truth I was grappling with. Immortality. A thousand-year-old secret. And I, caught in the middle of it, with no way out.

Poggin's jowls quivered as he joined in the laughter. "If what you say is true—that no one can live beyond two hundred years—then why do so many people scream 'Long live the Emperor' until their voices go hoarse? Why the obsession with immortality?"

I forced myself to stay calm, refusing to rise to his bait. "Only the insane would demand such absurdities from others."

Mark turned to Poggin, his tone casual, as if discussing the weather. "It seems he's determined not to believe us. Our plans won't be derailed by him, though. I think it's time we ended this."

Poggin's smile didn't waver. "Go ahead. He's caused me enough trouble. I won't shed any tears for him."

I quickly pointed at Luna, my voice sharp and accusing. "And you, Mrs. Xi? You knew from the very beginning who the victim was and who the murderer was, didn't you? How could you treat your husband's killer as your own?"

She met my gaze with icy detachment. "I'll become the richest woman in the world. My husband is dead—what does it matter if he stays that way?"

I couldn't help but slap my own forehead in frustration. Now I understood. From the very start, I had been ensnared in a trap meticulously laid by Mark Xi and Luna. And with every step, I had only sunk deeper.

Clenching my fists, I took a step toward Mark. Even if I couldn't kill him, I could at least make him feel some pain. But before I could reach him, he did something utterly bizarre.

He drew a razor-sharp dagger from his belt—not to attack me, but to plunge it into his own arm.

The blade sank deep into his flesh with a sickening *thunk*. Yet he didn't flinch. Instead, he waved his arm casually, as if nothing had happened. "You see? We've even lost the ability to feel pain."

I stood frozen, my fists loosening involuntarily. I had been ready to beat him senseless, but how could I hurt someone who felt no pain? Someone who could stab himself without so much as a wince?

As I watched him pull the dagger free, no blood flowed from the wound. The gash closed almost instantly, leaving no trace. My voice sounded foreign to my own ears as I asked, "What... what is this? What have you become?"

Mark let out a sinister, cackling laugh. "I've already told you—the elixir of immortality!"

I muttered, half in disbelief, "The elixir of immortality?"

He nodded, his tone almost casual now, as if explaining something mundane. "Yes. If that term doesn't make sense to you, think of it as a super anti-aging serum."

I still didn't fully grasp it, but I noticed something: Mark Xi loved to show off. If I played dumb, he'd likely spill everything, eager to flaunt his knowledge. It wouldn't save me, but it would buy me time. And at the very least, I'd learn the truth before the end.

So I shrugged, feigning ignorance. "I still don't understand. Really, I don't."

Mark smirked. "I can explain it to you."

But Luna cut in sharply, "He's stalling for time. Can't you see that?"

Mark waved her off. "Of course I see it. But what does it matter? There's no one within three kilometers of here. Even if he drags this out for three days, all he's doing is prolonging his life by three days."

His words sent a chill through me. Three days? I doubted I had even three hours. But I had my plan. Every minute counted.

Mark continued, "If you want to understand my secret, I'll have to start from the beginning. Do you have the patience for that?"

I nodded. "Of course. My goal is to buy time. The more details, the better."

He chuckled. "I'll grant you this final wish. My disappearance—it happened because my speedboat was hit by artillery fire from the shore. Shrapnel tore into my shoulder. In the chaos, I grabbed onto a piece of driftwood and floated out to sea.

"The wound was severe. I lost consciousness not long after I started drifting. When I woke up, I was in a canoe.

"And in that canoe were the three of them."

Mark paused, gesturing toward the three natives standing silently nearby. I had assumed they were merely Poggin's servants, but now I realized they had known Mark long before this moment.

He continued, his voice taking on a storyteller's cadence. "The canoe drifted aimlessly at sea. I was certain I wouldn't survive. Then, one of the three natives picked up a bamboo tube and motioned for me to open my mouth. Inside the tube was a milky-white liquid. At the time, I had no idea what it was, but I obeyed and drank two mouthfuls. The taste was bitter, almost unbearable. I nearly spat it out.

"But within a minute, something miraculous happened. The pain vanished. The wound on my shoulder began to heal at an incredible rate. Even the shrapnel embedded in my muscle seemed to be pushed out by some mysterious force. I'm certain no surgeon in the world could have treated a wound so effectively in such a short time.

"In that moment, I knew I would survive. And more than that, I realized this milky liquid was some kind of miraculous native medicine. If I could discover its formula or obtain it in large quantities, I would become the richest man in the world. Was there any doubt about that?"

I couldn't help but interject coldly, "It just proves how inherently greedy you are."

He didn't take offense, merely smiling. "You can say that. But isn't everyone greedy by nature? I stayed on that canoe until we reached a small island. It was a truly isolated place—no more than three acres of barren rock. Yet, from the cracks in those rocks grew a strange plant.

"The plant's stem resembled bamboo, but it bore enormous fruit. When the fruit ripened, squeezing its skin would release the same milky liquid the natives had given me on the canoe. During my time on that desolate island, I drank that liquid every day."

Mark paused for a moment, his eyes gleaming with a fervor that bordered on madness. "Gradually," he continued, "I discovered something extraordinary. The island was home to about a hundred inhabitants. There were no children, no elderly—just adults in their prime. They ventured out to sea to fish, braving the fiercest storms, yet they always returned unharmed. Eventually, I realized the truth: they were immortal. The liquid extracted from the fruit on that island was *the elixir of immortality*—a super anti-aging serum, an unparalleled regenerative agent for the human body.

"I had stumbled upon a society of immortals! And by drinking the elixir, I had become one of them."

He paused again, his face flushed with excitement. He looked at me intently, as if gauging my reaction. "Do you know what aging agents are?" he asked rhetorically. "All living beings produce both aging agents and anti-aging agents during metabolism. Anti-aging agents suppress the growth and spread of aging. The life cycle of any organism is essentially a battle between these two forces. If anti-aging agents disappear from the body, a twelve-year-old child would biologically resemble an eighty-year-old man. Such cases are well-documented in medicine. Conversely, if the supply of anti-aging agents is continuously replenished, and the growth of aging agents is completely suppressed, then a person can achieve immortality!"

He spread his hands triumphantly. "I had discovered the secret to eternal life!"

I was stunned into silence. Mark's words sounded too fantastical to be true, yet his conviction was undeniable. Could there really be an "elixir of immortality" in this world? It was almost impossible to believe. For now, all I could do was listen and try to piece together the truth.

Mark went on, "After this revelation, I began collecting as much of the white liquid as I could. It took me four years to gather a large barrel of it and build a massive canoe. By then, I had no idea the war had ended, so I was still hesitant to leave. But I knew that once I returned to the civilized world, I could sell this elixir in small vials and become unimaginably wealthy. Finally, I set out to sea in my canoe. On the twentieth day, I encountered Poggin.

"Poggin was already a successful businessman by then. His yacht was speeding through the water when it collided with my canoe, sending my precious barrel of elixir sinking into the ocean. But Poggin rescued me and brought me back to the civilized world. Isn't that right, Poggin?"

The portly Poggin nodded solemnly, his expression unreadable.

Mark continued, his tone shifting to one of frustration and determination. "I told Poggin about my incredible experience, but he laughed at me, calling me a madman. He claimed to know every island in the South Pacific like the back of his hand, yet he insisted no such island existed. I didn't bother arguing with him. When we reached Timor, he tried to hand me over to the American military authorities, but I escaped. I stole one of his yachts and set out to return to that island."

The pieces of the puzzle were finally starting to come together. I remained silent, but my mind raced. What could I do in this situation? How could I turn this to my advantage?

Mark waved his hand dramatically as he went on. "But when I tried to find the island again, it was as if it had vanished from the sea. I sailed to the coordinates I remembered, only to find endless ocean. I ran out of fuel, and as my yacht drifted, I was rescued once again by Poggin. This time, he brought me into his... organization."

I couldn't help but interject, "What kind of organization?"

Poggin smirked, his expression oily and self-satisfied. "No harm in telling you now. A smuggling ring."

I wasn't surprised. In a colonial outpost like this, someone with Poggin's wealth and influence was almost certainly involved in illegal activities. I sneered, "How fitting. The two of you are a perfect match."

Neither of them seemed bothered by my jab. In fact, they looked almost proud of themselves.

Mark carried on, undeterred. "Years later, I finally rediscovered the island. To reach it, you have to navigate a treacherous ring of waters—a place feared by sailors for its violent storms and swarms of tiger sharks, sawfish, and swordfish. But once a year, for just a few hours, the waters calm. That's how I managed to drift out the first time—I happened to hit that brief window of calm."

I couldn't resist a sarcastic remark. "Lucky you."

Mark smirked shamelessly, his arrogance oozing from every word. "My luck has always been good, and it's only just beginning. I will become an idol to the entire world, the wealthiest man alive, because I hold the secret to immortality. I'll sit at home, and money will flood in like a tidal wave!"

I was stunned into silence. He was right. If what he claimed was true, wealth would indeed pour in uncontrollably. Who wouldn't want to live forever, especially the rich and powerful? Death, after all, is the great equalizer—it comes for everyone, rich or poor. But now, Mark and Poggin claimed to have shattered that inevitability. The world's elite would gladly hand over half their fortunes for the chance to extend their lives indefinitely.

Admittedly, the idea of a supernatural anti-aging serum, an "elixir of immortality," sounded absurd. And Mark and Poggin were far from honorable men—they were despicable, repulsive even. But objectively speaking, their business wasn't inherently unethical. They had discovered this miraculous substance on a remote island and were selling it. No matter how exorbitant the price, it could be seen as a fair transaction.

Yet, this raised a new question in my mind: Why were they so desperate to keep this a secret? Why had they decided to kill me the moment I stumbled upon their operation?

The puzzle deepened, and I couldn't shake the feeling that there was more to their story—something darker, more sinister, lurking beneath the surface.

I pondered for a moment before asking, "If this is a legitimate business, why do you need to silence me?"

Poggin, Mark, and Lunag exchanged glances, their faces twisting into sly, knowing smiles. Yet none of them spoke a word.

Immediately, I realized there was another layer to this—a deeper, more dangerous secret about the "elixir of immortality." That secret was the reason they couldn't let me live.

But what was it?

My intense concentration must have caught their attention, because Mark chuckled darkly. "Don't bother thinking about it. You'll never figure it out. Your time is up, my friend."

As he spoke, his grin turned menacing, sending a chill down my spine.

I quickly raised my hand, trying to stall. "Wait! You still haven't explained why you killed your brother after he went to such lengths to find you."

Mark's thick eyebrows shot up, and his face contorted with anger. But before he could respond, Luna cut in sharply, "Don't tell him. Why should he know so much?"

I turned to her, but she averted her gaze, refusing to meet my eyes. That told me everything I needed to know. There was some tangled, dark history between her, Brian, and Mark—a secret they were desperate to keep buried.

Mark stepped closer, clapping his hands. Another native approached, carrying a tray. On it lay a gleaming, razor-sharp curved blade, resembling a sickle. Mark picked it up, his smile turning cruel.

I raised my hand again, trying to buy time. "Wait! I have one more question. You have to answer this one."

Mark laughed, a cold, mirthless sound. "Fine. A dying man's last question. Go ahead."

In truth, this question was crucial, but I also had an ulterior motive for asking it now. When I saw him summon the native and take the blade, a flicker of hope ignited within me. If he had chosen to shoot me, I would have had no chance of survival. But by opting to kill me with a blade—likely to flaunt his supposed invincibility—he had made a fatal mistake. Overconfidence often leads to stupidity, and his arrogance was about to give me an opening.

Of course, after years of consuming the "elixir," he likely believed himself impervious to harm. A blade in his hands was just another way to assert his dominance. But the key difference was this: a gun would have left me no room to escape, while a blade—no matter how sharp—gave me a fighting chance.

I took two steps forward, positioning myself behind a sofa, my hand resting on its back. Then I asked, "If you're truly immortal, why were you afraid of the electric chair?"

Mark glanced at me sideways, a sly grin spreading across his face. "What do you think? Are you trying to find my weakness? Do you believe electricity can kill me?"

I glared at him, my anger boiling over. "But you used a despicable lie to trick me into breaking you out of death row!"

"That's right," he admitted shamelessly. "I'm immortal, so the electric chair couldn't kill me. But what do you think would happen if they discovered they couldn't execute me?"

I didn't answer. The truth was, nothing like this had ever happened before. There had never been someone the electric chair couldn't kill. How could I possibly know what would happen to such a person?

Mark continued, his voice dripping with mockery. "They'd sentence me to life imprisonment—on paper, at least. In reality,

I'd become a lab rat. They'd probably dissect me piece by piece to figure out why I couldn't die. That's why I needed you to break me out."

I pointed at the gleaming curved blade in his hand. "And this is how you repay me, is it?"

He sneered. "You brought this on yourself. If you hadn't been so nosy, you'd have reaped the rewards when I became wealthy. My fortune will be vast enough to build my own kingdom, or fund a coup to install myself as the shadow ruler. If you'd stayed in line, you could have found sanctuary in my domain, free from any pursuers."

I spread my hands in mock resignation. "Too bad I couldn't play along. I couldn't stand being deceived, so here we are. Right?"

Mark tilted his head, his expression cold. "Exactly."

He took another step toward me, and I stood my ground, my heart pounding. I had already assessed the situation. If I could roll out of the way before Poggin, Luna, or Mark drew their guns, I might be able to crash through the door and escape the hall.

Once outside, I'd be surrounded by dark mountains and dense forests. My enemies would no longer be these three immortals but the venomous snakes and wild beasts lurking in the shadows.

But could I make it to the door?

Mark took another step closer. My hands gripped the back of the sofa tightly.

He advanced again, and the glint of the sharp blade in his hand was so bright it stung my eyes. In that moment, I pushed the sofa forward with all my strength.

The sofa was mounted on four casters, designed for easy movement. Normally, this feature was for comfort, but now it was my lifeline.

The sofa, mounted on casters, shot forward with tremendous speed and force as I pushed it, slamming directly into Mark. I didn't wait to see the result. The moment the sofa left my hands, I sprang backward, executing a swift backflip—a move honed by years of relentless training in Chinese martial arts.

In less than two seconds, I had flipped to the door. I slammed it open, dashed through the hallway, and burst through the front entrance. Just as I did, two spears whistled through the air toward me. I dropped to the ground, feeling the spears graze my back as they embedded themselves in the doorframe ahead.

I scrambled to my feet, leaped outside, and yanked the spears free. They would serve as both weapons and tools— essential for surviving in the wilderness, where I expected to spend some time.

Once I was outside, I knew I was safe—for now.

I sprinted toward the darkest part of the forest and dropped to the ground, lying still. The shadows enveloped me, and I waited, my heart pounding, ready for whatever came next.

CHAPTER 8

The Hidden Paradise

I immediately heard Mark and Poggin cursing from inside the house, followed by the sporadic sound of gunfire. I stayed low, motionless. Their shots were wild and aimless, and since bullets don't have eyes, there was no chance they'd hit me.

Poggin's voice, filled with rage, cut through the chaos. "I'll go back and bring the hounds. We'll search the entire island."

Mark responded, "Yes, hurry. If we don't, our plans will be ruined."

Even now, I couldn't understand why they were so desperate to eliminate me or why they were convinced I would ruin their plans. If I were to reveal everything I'd witnessed to the world, it would essentially serve as free advertising for their anti-aging serum. People would be more inclined to believe in the elixir's life-extending properties. Yet, they were determined to kill me.

What other secrets did the elixir hold?

At that moment, I couldn't figure it out. My mind was too preoccupied with survival. My immediate priority was to escape. I needed to find a stream or river, cross it multiple times, and throw off the scent of the hounds.

I crept backward, moving quietly until I felt I was at a safe distance. Then I broke into a run, tumbling down a slope before getting back on my feet and continuing forward. Eventually, I reached a mountain stream.

The water was deep, almost up to my neck. I swam across, then back, repeating the process five or six times. After the final crossing, I climbed onto the opposite bank and kept running.

When I could no longer run, I walked. When even walking became impossible, I used the two spears as crutches, dragging myself forward until my body gave out and I collapsed.

I fell to the ground, rolling a few times until I was behind a large rock. There, I finally caught my breath.

As dawn broke, I began to see my surroundings clearly. I was lying in a valley surrounded by high mountains, dense trees, and unfamiliar tropical plants. Looking back the way I'd come, there was no trace of my path.

And so far, I hadn't heard any barking. That meant the hounds hadn't picked up my scent.

I was safe—for now.

Using the sharp edge of one of the spears, I cut two large leaves, each the size of a taro leaf. They were big enough to cover my entire body. I lay down beneath them and closed my eyes.

I was exhausted. I needed rest, even if I couldn't sleep.

Sleep, however, was impossible. My mind was a whirlwind of thoughts.

What should I do next? I had uncovered most of Poggin and Mark's secrets. Should I try to make it back to civilization and alert the authorities that Mark was a fugitive? But I quickly dismissed the idea.

It was useless. Poggin's influence here was immense. He could easily protect Mark, and given his apparent lack of conscience, he might even be pleased to see Mark eliminated.

So, what should I do?

Build a raft and escape? The idea was laughable. Right now, all I could focus on was surviving—avoiding being eaten by wild animals, evading Poggin and Mark, and not starving to death. In short, I needed to stay alive.

Only by staying alive could I accomplish anything.

I lay there until noon, drifting into a fitful sleep. After a short rest, I woke and continued walking. Along the way, I picked and ate any fruit that looked edible.

I kept moving forward, hoping to reach the sea. If I could make it to the coast, my chances of survival might improve.

But by nightfall, there was still no sign of the ocean.

As darkness fell, exhaustion weighed heavily on me. The last few miles had been fraught with venomous snakes, so I didn't dare sleep. I forced myself to keep walking, pausing only to sit on clean rocks, staying alert.

By midnight, the world was pitch black. I leaned against a tree, my eyelids heavy, struggling to stay awake.

Just then, I saw a flicker of light in the trees ahead.

My heart leapt. I pressed myself against the tree, motionless, and raised my spear. The light was from a torch.

A torch doesn't move on its own—someone was holding it. Was it Poggin and Mark's search party?

If it was, I was in serious trouble.

I stared ahead. The torchlight flickered but didn't move closer, and there were no unusual sounds. Gradually, I relaxed.

If it were a search party, they would be making noise, not moving in silence. So, who was it? Another escapee like me?

The thought made me grimace. This place housed many hardened criminals, so it wasn't surprising if one or two had escaped. But the idea of joining forces with a fugitive was unsettling.

I steadied myself and crept forward cautiously.

The torch remained in the same spot, suggesting the holder hadn't noticed me. When I was about seven or eight steps away, I stopped and peered ahead.

It was indeed a person holding the torch—a single individual.

The man was short, with dark brown skin, a large head, and thick, curly hair. He wore nothing but a cloth around his waist and carried a bamboo tube at his side. He was a native.

The native was crouched on the ground, holding the torch in one hand and digging vigorously with the other. He had already dug a small pit but continued to work tirelessly.

The native looked similar to those I had seen at Poggin's house and villa. This observation made me hesitate to call out to him.

If my guess was correct, this native had also lived for an unknown number of years, sustained by the super anti-aging serum. I didn't want to alert him, as he might be allied with Poggin and Mark.

I watched him silently, unsure of what he was doing. He kept digging with such intensity that, after a while, I heard a faint squeaking sound from the ground. The native suddenly straightened up.

It was then that I realized what he was doing. In his hand was a fat field mouse. What followed was even more revolting. He used a blunt knife to stab at the mouse's neck.

The knife was too dull to penetrate easily, and the mouse writhed and squealed in agony. Finally, the mouse died, and the native roughly skinned it, holding it over the torch to roast. He began eating it almost raw, without waiting for it to cook properly.

As I watched him devour the mouse, I became certain he wasn't one of Poggin's allies.

If he were, no matter how hungry he was, he could have waited to return to the villa for a proper meal. He wouldn't be here, practically eating a field mouse alive. Convinced of this, I decided to reveal myself. I took a step forward.

My left foot landed on a dry branch, producing a loud *crack*. The sound made the native jump to his feet, immediately pointing his small knife at me.

I didn't know whether he was hostile or friendly, so I quickly aimed my spear at him.

We stood there, locked in a tense standoff for a full two minutes.

During that time, I kept a smile on my face, though my facial muscles began to ache from the effort.

Finally, the native's wary expression softened, and he smiled back at me.

When a civilized person smiles at you, you might remain cautious. But when a native smiles, it's genuine. Relieved, I lowered my spear first.

The native also lowered his knife and pushed the half-cooked field mouse toward me. I politely declined. As he resumed eating, I tried to communicate with him.

I attempted several languages commonly spoken in the South Pacific islands, but he didn't understand any of them. However, he seemed very interested in my spear. He pointed at it and repeatedly said, "Han Tong Jia," "Han Tong Jia."

I had no idea what "Han Tong Jia" meant. I used gestures to indicate that I wanted to go to the sea.

It took at least an hour, combined with drawings on the ground, for him to understand my intention.

In turn, he spent some time making me understand that he also wanted to go to the sea.

I realized that simple drawings and gestures were our best means of communication. Over the next hour, I learned that he had escaped from the villa.

He drew a house on the ground—this native had a surprising talent for art. The house had a distinctive pointed roof, unmistakably Poggin's villa. Then he drew a small figure leaving the house.

He pointed at the figure and then at himself. I drew another small figure next to his, holding two spears, and pointed at it, then at myself, indicating that I, too, had escaped from the villa.

He looked at me with a strange expression, clearly asking why I had escaped.

I couldn't answer that. The situation was too complex to convey through drawings.

He patted the bamboo tube at his waist and gave me that same suspicious look. I didn't know what was inside the tube, so I returned his gaze with equal suspicion. After a moment of hesitation, he opened the tube.

Inside was a milky-white liquid, emitting a strong, indescribable odor. I only caught a glimpse before he quickly sealed the tube again, clearly valuing its contents. My heart skipped a beat. I immediately recalled Mark's words—this milky liquid was the "elixir of immortality"!

I looked at the native. He brought the tube to his lips, mimed drinking, then shook his head. He pointed at the villa, spread his hands, and finally rolled his eyes, standing still like a wooden statue for a moment before pointing at the running figure again.

I understood that he was explaining why he had fled, but I couldn't decipher the meaning behind his series of gestures. He mimed drinking the elixir, then pointed at Poggin's villa and shook his head. This likely meant that Poggin had denied him the elixir. But what did his wide-eyed, statue-like pose signify?

I asked him repeatedly, and he repeated the gestures, but I couldn't make sense of them. Eventually, I gave up and invited him to join me in heading to the sea. He seemed pleased and then drew a small island on the ground, pointing at it and saying, "Han Tong Jia!"

Finally, I understood. "Han Tong Jia" was the name of the island. He was inviting me to go there with him.

My mind raced. If he was from that island, he must have experience with navigation. He would be the perfect guide to help me escape. Moreover, "Han Tong Jia" was the source of the elixir. I needed to investigate it. Perhaps there, I could uncover the secrets of the "elixir of immortality."

So, I quickly nodded in agreement.

That night, we continued communicating through drawings and gestures, exchanging many ideas. The next day, we set off together. I knew that on an island, if you kept walking in one direction, you would eventually reach the sea. Using this method, the native and I arrived at the coastline.

The beach was covered in sand as white as flour, scattered with beautiful seashells. The smallest were no bigger than a finger, while the largest could have served as a bed for the native.

We lay on the sand for a while, then began to plan our next steps.

Over the next three days, we cut down about ten trees and used vines to tie them into several rafts. We also fashioned wooden barrels to store fresh water from the mountain stream. I gathered plenty of fruit and caught over a dozen large crabs, tying them to the raft. Those crabs would be enough to feed us for a month.

Then, we pushed the raft into the sea, riding the outgoing tide as it carried us south.

The raft drifted on the ocean for seven long days.

Surviving on a raft and hoping to reach a specific island seemed nearly impossible, but the native remained optimistic. Every time the moon rose, he couldn't help but cheer.

On the seventh night, he began pulling seaweed from the water and tasting the seawater—his way of determining our location. Then, he picked up a large conch shell and blew into it with all his might.

The conch emitted a monotonous, mournful sound. He blew it for hours, until my head was spinning. Finally, I heard a distant reply—a similar sound echoing back.

I couldn't help but cheer at his ingenious method of calling for help. The distant sound grew closer, and soon, I saw several canoes approaching.

It was sunrise. The canoes moved swiftly, and in no time, they were upon us.

There were three canoes, each carrying three natives who looked just like my companion.

My friend—after nearly half a month together, I could certainly call him that—shouted and spoke rapidly, his words firing like a machine gun.

The natives in the canoes responded in the same language. We boarded one of the canoes, and immediately, a native handed me a large bamboo tube, uncorking it and offering it to me.

Inside was the milky-white elixir of immortality!

Over the past two weeks, I had watched my friend drink the elixir every day. He was careful, taking only a sip or two at a time, never more. While I didn't harbor any delusions of immortality, I was curious to try it. I hadn't asked him for any, but I couldn't help thinking he was being stingy.

Now, with a whole tube of the elixir offered to me, I was eager to taste it.

I smiled at the native who handed me the tube, expressing my thanks. But suddenly, my friend shouted and snatched the tube from my hands. He moved so quickly that a large portion of the milky liquid spilled out.

He glared at me, shaking his head vigorously.

His meaning was crystal clear—he didn't want me to drink the elixir.

At that moment, I couldn't help but feel a surge of anger. It was one thing for him to refuse to share the elixir from his own bamboo tube, but to snatch away what someone else had offered me was going too far.

My anger stemmed, of course, from knowing that this milky liquid was the real "elixir of immortality." I had witnessed its miraculous effects firsthand. Naturally, I wanted to drink some, to become immune to gunshot wounds and live forever!

So, without thinking, I let out an angry shout and reached out to grab the tube back. But at that moment, the native suddenly shoved me hard.

The push came out of nowhere. I had come to think of him as "my friend," so I didn't expect him to turn on me so abruptly. The force of his shove sent me stumbling backward, nearly falling out of the canoe.

The native began shouting in a strange, guttural voice, waving his arms as if giving a speech to the others in the canoe. It was then that I realized this native—my so-called friend—held a high status among his people.

As he gesticulated wildly, like an overzealous leader, the others listened in silence.

The canoe continued to glide forward, but suddenly, the roar of a massive wave drowned out his voice.

The native seemed to finish his speech, pointing at me. Before I could comprehend what was happening, a towering wave and four natives lunged at me simultaneously.

If the four natives had reached me first, I might have been able to fend them off. But the wave hit first.

The wave was enormous, powerful, and relentless. In an instant, the calm, blue sea turned into a frothing, gray-black monster, like a pack of ravenous wolves charging at me.

Of course, the wave wasn't targeting me alone—it was crashing into the entire canoe. In less than a tenth of a second, the canoe was completely submerged.

The suddenness of it all left me dizzy and disoriented, unsure of what to do.

At that moment, the four natives tackled me.

They pinned me down, their arms wrapping tightly around different parts of my body while their other hands seemed to grip the canoe.

I didn't struggle because I knew they meant no harm.

They were holding onto me to keep me from being swept away by the waves. Even if they had meant me harm, I wouldn't have been able to resist—the waves were too violent.

I felt my body shrink, as small as a peanut, being tossed up and down relentlessly.

This dizzying sensation lasted for half an hour. I couldn't even tell if I had vomited during that time because I was in a semi-conscious state.

I had plenty of experience with the ocean, but this storm was unlike anything I'd ever encountered. Each wave felt like it was trying to rip my internal organs out of my body, making it unbearable.

When I finally regained consciousness, I could still feel the relentless up-and-down motion, but at least I was no longer being held down. I moved my hands slightly and suddenly felt something solid—dirt!

For someone who had just endured such a violent storm, the sudden sensation of dirt beneath my hands was indescribably joyful. I clutched the soil tightly, pushed myself up, and sat upright.

In that moment, the dizziness vanished. I opened my eyes and was greeted by a lush, vibrant green. I was on the beach of a stunningly beautiful island.

The green came from the sea, so calm it almost seemed like a piece of still green jade.

But looking further out, I could see a gray-black border surrounding the calm waters, constantly churning and shifting.

I immediately understood—that was where I had just encountered the storm. This island was perpetually encircled by massive waves, with only brief periods of calm each year. That explained why it remained a hidden paradise.

I shifted my gaze from the horizon and noticed several natives standing nearby. They all looked similar, but I could still pick out my friend among them.

As I recognized him, he walked toward me. In that moment, I wasn't sure whether to continue treating him as a friend or to ignore him, given how he had treated me on the canoe.

The native stopped beside me and pointed forward, gesturing for me to stand and follow.

As I got to my feet, I swayed slightly, and he reached out to steady me.

It seemed he was still friendly toward me. I decided not to hold a grudge, but now that I was on the island, I was determined to try the milky liquid.

I followed the group of natives as they led me forward. The island wasn't densely forested, as Mark had mentioned—most of it was rocky. But the rocks were strangely shaped and beautifully colored, making the entire island look like a scene from a fairy tale. The most abundant plants were giant bamboo-like structures.

However, these bamboo-like plants weren't actual bamboo.

I noticed they bore grayish-white flowers and clusters of fruit, which were undoubtedly the source of the elixir.

Walking from the beach to a mountain hollow, I estimated that the sheer number of fruits produced by these plants could sustain the island's population indefinitely.

The natives seemed to rely on these fruits as their primary food and drink. Each of them carried a large bamboo tube at their waist, occasionally opening it to take a few sips of the liquid inside.

I was led to a spacious bamboo house, tall and airy, with a cool, refreshing atmosphere inside. After a while, someone brought me a large plate of food.

The plate was filled with fish, shrimp, and a particularly plump and delicious clam. Seizing the opportunity, I pointed at the native's bamboo tube, gesturing for him to share some of its contents with me.

But the native immediately stepped back, avoiding my request, and quickly left the bamboo house.

His reaction infuriated me. I couldn't help but shout in frustration and stormed out of the house.

As soon as I stepped outside, I saw my friend rushing toward me. To my shock, he was carrying a submachine gun.

For a moment, I had no idea what was happening. I quickly retreated back into the bamboo house, but the native followed me inside. His next actions, however, put me at ease. He placed the gun on the ground and gestured for me to pick it up.

I bent down and picked up the submachine gun, inspecting it carefully.

The gun was clearly a relic from World War II, but it was in good condition and loaded, ready to fire. The native pointed at the gun and made a series of gestures, asking if I knew how to use it.

I nodded, and he looked pleased.

I still didn't understand his intentions, but at that moment, I heard the sound of drums. Looking outside, I saw many natives rushing out of their houses and gathering in the open area in front.

The native crouched on the ground and used a bamboo stick to draw a fish-like shape in the dirt. The shape was clearly underwater. Inside it, he drew two figures, both holding guns. Then, he drew an island, indicating that these two people would come ashore. One of the figures had a large, round belly.

At first, it was hard to understand what he was trying to convey, but by now, it was crystal clear. He had drawn a small submarine, and the figure with the big belly was undoubtedly Poggin.

The meaning of his drawing was obvious: Poggin and Mark would arrive on the island in a submarine, armed with guns.

And his reason for giving me the submachine gun was equally clear—he wanted me to deal with Poggin and Mark!

Once I fully understood his meaning, I nodded, pointed at the two figures he had drawn, and raised the gun to signal that I could handle them.

But at the same time, a new question arose in my mind.

The people on this island drank the "elixir of immortality" daily, granting them extraordinary powers and making them immune to bullets. So why were they afraid of Poggin and Mark arriving with guns?

Mark had lived on this island for several years, so the natives surely knew he was bulletproof. Why, then, did the native want me to use the submachine gun against them?

I tried to voice my doubts, but it took a long time to make him understand.

Finally, when he grasped my question, he grabbed my arm and pulled me outside.

We left the bamboo house and found many people gathered in the open area. The drums continued to beat slowly and rhythmically. I estimated there were about three hundred natives.

Notably, there were no elderly or children among them—everyone appeared to be around thirty years old.

Seeing this, a thought struck me: the milky liquid was indeed a powerful anti-aging serum, capable of extending life indefinitely. However, it must also destroy reproductive capabilities. Otherwise, the island's population wouldn't be three hundred—it would be three million. The complete absence of children was proof that the islanders had lost their ability to reproduce.

As I pondered this, the native continued to pull me along.

I didn't know where he was taking me, but after a long walk, we reached a hilltop. There, four large, square stones formed a square enclosure, with a flat stone slab covering the top.

The native walked up to the stones, lifted the slab, and gestured for me to come closer and look inside.

My heart filled with curiosity, but I approached anyway.

When I reached the stones, I was stunned. What I saw wasn't particularly unusual, but it was something I never expected to find on this island.

I saw a dead body.

CHAPTER 9

Elixir's Side Effects

The man was undoubtedly dead, though he looked as if he were merely asleep. He was a native, with dark brown skin and curly hair, sitting in a serene posture. However, there were two dark holes in his chest.

I had brought the submachine gun with me, and the native pointed at the gun's muzzle, then at the holes in the dead man's chest, his face filled with terror.

I immediately understood.

The natives on this island might not realize that the "elixir of immortality" they drank daily could lead them to eternal life. They probably didn't even understand the concept of death. So, when one of them died, it naturally filled them with fear.

And I knew exactly how this man had died—he had been shot by a submachine gun.

If the bullets had hit any other part of his body, he might have felt nothing. But if the bullets pierced his heart, he would die. In other words, those who consumed the elixir weren't invincible. They had a fatal weakness: the heart.

Of course, Mark knew this. This man might have been killed by Mark himself!

The reason Mark had begged me to break him out of death row was now clear. When high-voltage electricity passes through the body, it inevitably causes cardiac arrest.

In other words, the electric chair could kill Mark!

That's why he had been so desperate, so convincingly like a man on the brink of death. It was one of the reasons I had been fooled.

I took a step back, and together with the native, we replaced the stone slab. I nodded to show I understood how to kill Poggin and Mark.

The native and I walked back down the hill. Along the way, I deliberately patted the bamboo tube at his waist, but he immediately shifted it to the other side.

I thought to myself that these islanders might be inherently cunning.

They wanted to use me to deal with Mark and Poggin but refused to share the milky liquid with me.

Feeling displeased, I patted his shoulder. When he turned to look at me, I raised the gun, pointed at his bamboo tube, and then threw the submachine gun to the ground!

My message was clear: if he wouldn't give me the "elixir of immortality," I wouldn't use the gun to help him against Poggin and Mark.

My actions were undeniably underhanded. After all, dealing with Poggin and Mark wasn't entirely unrelated to me. But at that moment, convinced that the natives were cunning, I decided to use this opportunity to pressure him.

The native immediately looked flustered, his face filled with extreme distress.

I stood with my hands on my hips, waiting for his response, all the while silently cursing him for dragging this out.

Solving this issue should have been simple for him. All he had to do was let me drink the elixir, and I would no longer threaten him. Yet, it was clear he had no intention of doing so.

To make sure he understood, I pointed at the bamboo tube on his waist again.

He gave a bitter smile, pointed at the tube, mimed drinking from it, then stretched out his arm, stiffened his body, and froze in place.

He had made this gesture several times before, but I had never understood its meaning.

I had pondered over what this gesture could signify, but it remained a mystery. Even now, I still didn't fully grasp it. However, his repeated use of this gesture at least clarified one thing: it was the reason he refused to let me drink the "elixir of immortality."

Could it be that drinking the elixir would cause someone to drop dead on the spot? If he thought such a childish lie could fool me, it only fueled my anger further.

I firmly pointed at the bamboo tube on his waist again. This time, he began pacing in circles, beads of sweat forming on his dark brown face.

I thought to myself, *I'm close to succeeding!*

But at the same time, I couldn't understand why he was so anxious. On this island, the milky liquid was a naturally abundant resource—limitless and inexhaustible. It wasn't precious, much like the seawater surrounding the island.

Why was he being so stingy, so adamant about not letting me drink it? Moreover, it seemed that, at his instruction, none of the natives were willing to share the "elixir of immortality" with me.

This was one of the reasons I was so furious.

I remained standing still, and the native suddenly crouched down. He began speaking in a language I couldn't understand while drawing on the ground.

First, he drew a person tilting their head back to drink from a bamboo tube. Then, the tube disappeared from the person's hand, indicating they had stopped drinking the elixir. Finally, he drew a third figure lying on the ground.

These three drawings conveyed the same message as his earlier gestures, and it was equally infuriating. He was trying to convince me that drinking the elixir would kill me!

I glared at him and shook my head, signaling that there was no room for negotiation.

He grew increasingly frantic, pointing at the three figures he had drawn, then at himself. He lay down stiffly, his eyes wide open, and slowly sat up again. When he sat up, his eyes remained fixed, and his body seemed rigid.

In that flash of insight, I suddenly remembered something I had seen before.

What came to mind was the first time I had infiltrated Poggin's residence and entered a particular room. In that large room, I had seen many natives.

The natives I had seen in Poggin's house were clearly of the same origin as those on "Han Tong Jia" Island. They must have come from this island. Those natives had seemed almost lifeless, maintaining the same posture for long periods, like complete idiots.

Now, the native sitting rigidly on the ground looked exactly like those I had seen in Poggin's house.

As this realization hit me, I felt the need to reconsider the meaning of his gestures and drawings.

I carefully examined the three drawings again. The first showed a person drinking the elixir. The second depicted just a person. The third showed the person lying motionless on the ground. To emphasize this point, he had even demonstrated by lying stiffly on the ground himself.

This was clearly the key point he wanted to convey. But what did it mean? What was he trying to explain?

Suddenly, I understood!

It was a true epiphany. One second ago, I had been completely in the dark, filled with questions. But in the next second, it was as if an immense force had swept away all the fog, revealing the truth.

The native wasn't saying that drinking the "elixir of immortality" would lead to this outcome. He was saying that if you drank the elixir and then stopped, this would be the dire consequence!

Because there was this twist in the message, it had been harder for him to convey, which was why I hadn't understood earlier.

Now I understood. Long-term consumption of the elixir could indeed lead to immortality. But if you stopped—I didn't yet know for how long—you would become an idiot. You'd still be alive, but your brain would be utterly destroyed.

I had already seen this. The natives in Poggin's house had undoubtedly become like the living dead because they had been cut off from the elixir.

At the same time, I realized the true reason Poggin and Mark feared me.

The "elixir of immortality" they planned to sell required continuous consumption. If you stopped, you would turn into an idiot!

This was also why the native refused to let me drink the elixir.

Unless I stayed on this island forever, I would never have an uninterrupted supply of the elixir.

And for someone like me, from a civilized society, living on this island indefinitely was unimaginable. What would be the point of eternal life under such conditions?

Moreover, I suspected that the interval between doses of the elixir must be very short—perhaps only a few dozen hours. Mark had claimed that after leaving the island, he had spent years unable to find it again, but his words were clearly unreliable. Just as he had never mentioned the submarine they used to reach the island.

Additionally, after Mark was presumed murdered, a large bamboo tube had been found among his belongings. Of course, no one knew its purpose—it was for storing the "elixir of immortality."

This proved that he had never stopped drinking the elixir.

Even if he wasn't afraid of the electric chair, he had every reason to escape—because the elixir he carried with him was running out!

In that short span of time, I had pieced together so many answers, and my joy was indescribable.

I quickly helped my friend up from the ground and performed the islanders' traditional greeting.

He, of course, realized that I had finally understood his meaning, so he grinned broadly.

At that moment, I felt deeply ashamed. I had misjudged him as stingy and cunning, never imagining that he was so kind-hearted and had been looking out for me all along.

I picked up the gun and followed him back down the mountain to their village. Many natives were still gathered in the open area, waiting. My friend stepped into the crowd and began speaking loudly.

Only then did I realize that my friend was actually the ruler of the island—the leader of the natives!

His "speech" lasted about twenty minutes. I had no idea what he was saying, but I noticed he kept pointing in my direction.

When he finished speaking, all the natives suddenly turned and began bowing to me.

This unexpected honor left me flustered, unsure of how to respond.

Just then, a series of deafening gunshots erupted from the direction of the beach.

The seven or eight gunshots, amplified by the rocky terrain, echoed continuously, sounding even more terrifying. I froze in shock. My friend shouted a few commands, grabbed my arm, and led me to an enormous bamboo plant. He pointed at it, signaling for me to climb inside.

The "bamboo" was thick enough to hold me, and I realized that the gunshots must have come from Poggin or Mark—they had arrived!

They would never expect me to be on the island. Hiding here would make it much easier to deal with them.

I climbed into the bamboo and stood still.

The natives remained seated, the drumming continued, and many of them began bringing out large, sealed bamboo tubes. These tubes were undoubtedly filled with the elixir.

Half an hour later, another round of gunfire rang out, this time much closer.

I cautiously peeked out and saw Mark and Poggin.

Despite his size, Poggin moved surprisingly nimbly. Both men carried guns, but when the natives began bowing to them, they laughed triumphantly and set their weapons down.

The submachine guns now hung at their sides.

My friend had also hidden himself, and two other natives stepped forward. Mark actually spoke to them in their native language, and the two listened with great respect.

At that moment, I felt deeply conflicted.

If I were to suddenly attack, a single gunshot could send a bullet straight through their hearts. But I didn't want to do that—at the very least, I needed to capture Mark alive!

If I killed Mark, I would never be able to return home. How could I prove my innocence? The only way to clear my name was to bring him back alive. So, I had to force him to surrender his weapon, but that would be extremely difficult. Even though I was hidden in the bamboo and he had no idea I was there, I had to remember that I could only kill him by shooting him in the heart!

Mark, on the other hand, had no such limitations. If I made a sound and he turned around quickly, I would be in serious trouble.

He had no reason to fear me, and while I could only kill him by hitting his heart, he could shoot me anywhere to end my life.

If it were just Mark alone, I might have had a better chance. But he was with Poggin, and I couldn't possibly aim at both their hearts simultaneously.

So, I stayed hidden, unwilling to act rashly until I had a solid plan.

Mark continued to bark orders, his demeanor making it clear that he saw himself as the undisputed ruler of the island.

The natives' expressions showed their resentment, but they dared not speak out.

Seeing this, I couldn't help but sigh inwardly.

Mark should never have been able to dominate this island. The natives had all consumed the "elixir of immortality," and only a shot to the heart could kill them. If they rose up in rebellion, it would take only one or two sacrifices to completely subdue Mark.

But I believed that the dead man my friend had shown me was someone Mark had killed in front of all the natives. These islanders had no concept of "death." Suddenly witnessing someone becoming motionless, silent, and stiff must have filled them with unimaginable fear.

In such a state of terror, they could think of nothing but their fear. Of course, they wouldn't realize how easy it would be to resist Mark!

I sighed inwardly. Mark had only needed to kill one person to subjugate the entire island under his tyranny. He was undoubtedly a clever man.

As this thought crossed my mind, another idea struck me: if Mark could use the murder of one person to intimidate the entire island, could I do the same to subdue him?

Of course, I wouldn't shoot a native, but I could kill someone who deserved it.

That someone was Poggin.

I slowly raised my gun. At that moment, Poggin was standing beside Mark, his back to me, about twenty paces away. Shooting him in the heart would be effortless.

But before I pulled the trigger, I had to consider Mark's reaction.

Mark would undoubtedly grab his gun, turn around, and fire toward the source of the shot—my hiding place. What should I do then?

I didn't need long to figure it out.

Moreover, I realized I had to act immediately. Several natives were already glancing nervously toward my hiding spot, and their actions would surely draw Mark's attention. If he discovered me first, it would be disastrous.

I aimed the gun at Poggin's back. Shooting someone from behind was undeniably despicable, but I consoled myself with the thought that Poggin and Mark were equally vile. Using underhanded tactics against them didn't seem too unreasonable.

Only by thinking this way could I muster the courage to pull the trigger.

The gunshot rang out, startling everyone. All the natives jumped to their feet. Poggin turned around faster than Mark. A deep hole had appeared in his chest, but no blood flowed from the wound.

His face twisted into a strange expression—neither a cry nor a laugh. His mouth hung open as his body slowly crumpled to the ground, like a scene in slow motion.

Before his body hit the ground, Mark had already spun around. His reaction was exactly as I had anticipated—he immediately raised his gun, ready to fire toward my hiding spot.

But just as he lifted his weapon, my second shot rang out.

Another *bang* echoed, and my bullet struck the gun in his hands. Mark's arms jerked, and the gun fell to the ground, damaged beyond use.

Mark reacted quickly, stepping back to grab Bo Jin's gun. But at that moment, I pressed forward, leaping out of my hiding place.

As I emerged, Mark's face turned paler than a corpse. He must have thought I had died on Timor Island. My sudden appearance was something he could never have imagined!

My gun was aimed directly at his chest, and with Poggin already dead by my hand, Mark, being a clever man, didn't need me to say a word. He knew I had discovered the secret to killing him. So, he froze, raising his hands in surrender.

For the first time since he had deceived me, the anger that had been festering inside me finally found release.

I let out a series of cold laughs. To Mark, my laughter must have sounded cruel, because his body began to tremble. I said coldly, "Do you have anything to say?"

He stammered, "You're not going to kill me, are you? You don't want me to die on this island, do you?"

I had no intention of killing him, but since he thought so, I let him stew in his fear for a while longer, so I remained silent.

He continued to plead, "Poggin is dead. The secret of the elixir—only you and I know it now. We can use it to make a fortune. We can work together!"

I laughed. "Mr. Xi, I think your mind isn't quite clear. If I want to make a fortune, wouldn't it be better to do it alone rather than partnering with you?"

Mark was utterly desperate. The muscles on his face twitched, and I could see he was preparing to resist. I had to subdue him first.

As I considered how to communicate with the natives to have them restrain him, my friend appeared. Immediately, a large group of natives rushed forward, and in less than two minutes, Mark's body was tightly bound with tough wild vines.

I let out a sigh of relief, lowered my gun, and walked over to him. Mark was shouting, "You can't leave me here! You can't let these natives punish me! You have to take me with you!"

I nodded. "Indeed, I will take you with me. I'll take you back to death row."

To my surprise, Mark nodded eagerly. "Good! Good! But you have to keep supplying me with the elixir!"

I laughed. Now that I had completely subdued this cunning enemy, the relief and satisfaction in my heart were indescribable.

I sneered, "Of course. Before I hand you back to death row, I wouldn't want you to turn into a mindless idiot!"

Mark fell silent, as if he had been struck by a blow.

I continued, "But once you're back in your cell, I doubt your sister-in-law will send you any more elixir. Losing your senses before death—isn't that a good thing? Living with the knowledge of when you'll die isn't exactly pleasant, is it?"

Mark weakly replied, "You… you know everything now!"

I laughed heartily. "Of course I know everything. Come on, it's time to go!" I turned to "my friend" and gestured, trying to convey that I needed a canoe to take Mark and me away from the island.

After he understood my meaning, he simply glanced at Mark and didn't respond.

Under his gaze, Mark panicked and shouted, "Mr.Morris, you… you can't agree to leave me here!"

I deliberately said, "Leave you here? What's so bad about that? You'll have a constant supply of the elixir. You'll live forever. I believe these people are immortal, so they probably don't have the death penalty."

Mark gasped, "No, no! I'd rather go with you, back to the civilized world."

I said coldly, "This place is already civilized and peaceful. I think it was only after you arrived that things started to fall apart. Whatever punishment they have for you, I won't stop them. After they've punished you, I'll take you back."

Mark pleaded, "Stop toying with me. I'd rather go back and face the death penalty. Why are you tormenting me like this?"

I couldn't understand why he was so afraid. He had told me he couldn't feel pain, so what was he scared of? What kind of punishment would the natives inflict on him? I walked over to him and asked him directly.

Sweat dripped down his forehead. "Don't ask, please don't ask."

I said sternly, "No, I'm not only going to ask this question, but many others as well. Unless you answer them all, I'll leave you here."

Mark immediately gave in. Panting, he said, "On this island, there's a cave. Inside the cave is a pool filled with a kind of extremely vicious fish—a type of piranha. They'll submerge my legs in that pool!"

I sneered, "What's there to fear? You don't feel pain, and your muscles regenerate quickly."

Mark forced a bitter smile. "True, I don't feel pain, but watching my feet turn into bare bones over and over... No, you mustn't leave me here!"

Hearing this, I couldn't help but shudder. This kind of punishment sounded like something out of a myth, yet it was real. It was truly unbearable!

I turned to my friend and once again requested that he arrange a canoe to take Mark and me away. This time, the native nodded, but he walked over and spat on Mark's face before shouting orders. Perhaps because I insisted on taking Mark away, he was angry with me and ignored me.

However, the native leader's anger toward me didn't last long. Soon, he began gesturing to me again.

Two natives carried Mark, while I walked with my friend to the beach. When we arrived, a row of canoes was waiting. My friend personally boarded a relatively large canoe with wing-like supports on either side.

These supports would prevent the canoe from capsizing in rough waves. But remembering the massive waves I had encountered on my way here, I couldn't help but feel a sense of dread.

Before boarding the canoe, I didn't forget to ask my friend for a bamboo tube of the "elixir of immortality."

That tube of elixir, like Mark, was tied securely to the canoe. I didn't intend to use it for profit, but to keep Mark conscious

If he turned into an idiot, it would only create more trouble for me.

I had already planned my next steps. Once we left the island, I estimated we wouldn't drift at sea for too long. As soon as I was rescued, the first thing I would do was contact Flora, who was taking refuge at Mr. Miller's house, to let her know I was coming back. Everything could return to how it was before!

When you've been living a certain way for a long time, you don't always appreciate it. But once you lose it and then regain it, you realize how precious and wonderful that life truly is.

CHAPTER 10

Drinking the Elixir

Dozens of natives pushed the canoe into the sea. About twenty people were on board, and as soon as the canoe hit the water, a dozen paddles began rowing in unison, propelling us forward at great speed.

An hour later, the canoe reached the edge of the massive waves. The towering swells, rising and falling, seemed to freeze momentarily before collapsing, standing like solitary peaks in the middle of the ocean.

By this point, the canoe no longer needed to be paddled. The immense waves created a powerful whirlpool effect, pulling the canoe into a spinning motion as it surged toward the waves. Finally, we crashed into the heart of the swell.

From the moment the canoe entered the waves, everything felt like a nightmare. Just like on my journey here, I struggled at first, certain that if it weren't for the natives holding me down, I would have been thrown into the sea.

But before long, I passed out again.

When I woke up, we had escaped the ring of massive waves and were floating on calm waters.

"My friend" began untying two smaller canoes, clearly preparing to bid me farewell. I stood up, and he pointed to several bamboo tubes, indicating they contained fresh water.

He then pointed south, signaling that if we continued in that direction, we would reach land. The other natives erected a mast on my canoe and unfurled a sail.

These natives were natural sailors. Their sails were woven from fine vines, yet they were remarkably effective. They quickly adjusted the sail to catch the wind, and the canoe began moving south.

My friend shook my hand, and all the natives boarded the two smaller canoes, rowing away. They grew smaller and smaller until I could no longer see them.

I opened one of the bamboo tubes, took a sip of water, and poured some over my head. The salt crusted on my face was unbearable.

Mark, of course, didn't receive the same treatment. I simply poured a mouthful of the elixir into his mouth to prevent him from turning into an idiot due to the lack of continuous "anti-aging serum."

I lay down in the canoe as it continued sailing south, the bow splashing waves. I fell asleep, only to be awakened by Mark's shouts.

At first, I was startled and quickly sat up. Seeing that Mark was still tightly bound, I relaxed.

Mark's voice was shrill. "How long are we going to drift like this? You're so foolish! Poggin and I came here in a small submarine. Why didn't you use it?"

I sneered. "Why didn't you remind me when we were leaving?"

Mark retorted, "If I had reminded you, would you have listened?"

I immediately replied, "Of course not. There might have been others in the submarine. Why would I create more trouble for myself? I'd rather drift at sea for a few more days—"

As I spoke, I suddenly realized something and exclaimed, "Ah!" I hadn't used the submarine to escape because I wanted to avoid complications. But if there were others in the submarine, they would surely go ashore to investigate if Poggin didn't return.

Wouldn't that bring disaster to the natives on the island?

The moment this thought struck me, I wanted to shout and warn my friend. But when I opened my mouth, no sound came out. It was already too late. The natives were either struggling with the waves or had already returned to their island. Even if I shouted myself hoarse, they wouldn't hear me!

For a moment, I considered adjusting the sail to head back. But I knew I couldn't get the canoe through the massive waves. After hesitating, I asked, "Who else is in the submarine?"

A sly expression crept onto Mark's face. "There's one more person. He was the deputy commander of a Japanese submarine during World War II."

I stared at him for a moment. "You have a way to contact him, don't you?

You have a radio communicator on you, right?"

Mark nodded. "Yes, but if I'm going to contact him, you'll have to untie me first."

I studied him for a few more seconds. At this point, I didn't have a gun, and I was considering what I would do if he attacked me after being freed. I only thought about it briefly because I believed that even without a gun, I could still subdue him.

So, without saying anything more, I began untying him. The knots the natives had tied were intricate, and the vines were incredibly tough. No matter how hard I tried, I couldn't break them.

It took me quite some time to undo a few of the knots and loosen the vines. Mark slowly straightened up and reached into his right pants pocket.

In that instant, a thought struck me—Mark might have another weapon on him!

As soon as I realized this, I tensed, ready to lunge at him. But it was too late. Before I could move, Mark's hand emerged from his pocket, holding a pistol. I froze. I was no match for him, and on the canoe, there was no way to escape.

I was paralyzed, unsure of what to do in that moment. But Mark clearly knew his next move. He raised the gun and fired three shots at me in quick succession.

In the vast expanse of the ocean, the gunshots didn't sound particularly loud, but all three bullets hit me. I felt sharp pains in my shoulder and left leg. I couldn't stay upright and collapsed onto the boat.

My arm fell over the side, splashing seawater onto my wounds, intensifying the pain.

I gritted my teeth and shouted, "You beast! You damn beast! I should have left you on the island!"

Despite the three gunshot wounds, I struggled to get up.

But Mark kept his gun trained on my chest, preventing me from moving.

He said coldly, "Ash Morris, you're going to bleed to death."

Blood was steadily flowing from the three wounds on my shoulder and thigh. Mark's words were absolutely correct. If my situation didn't improve, I would lose consciousness from blood loss within thirty minutes.

But there was no way I could improve my situation.

Even if I risked being shot to subdue him now, what good would it do? I couldn't stop the bleeding from my three severe wounds.

Moreover, the pain from my injuries was overwhelming, and I suddenly felt the extreme fatigue that comes with approaching death. I no longer had the strength to fight him.

I just lay on the canoe, breathing heavily, my eyes wide open.

Mark laughed, his voice filled with malice. "There's a way for you to survive."

I asked weakly, "What... way?"

I had reached the end of my road. I felt an indescribable exhaustion, as if I just wanted to sleep. I wasn't even afraid of death anymore—I just wanted it to come quickly. Of course, I also desperately hoped to avoid it.

That's why I asked him in such a feeble voice.

Mark didn't answer directly. Instead, he opened a bamboo tube of the "elixir of immortality" and poured a small amount into another bamboo container.

He pushed the container toward me until it was right in front of me. "Drink it!"

I was stunned.

Mark continued, "Drink it, and your wounds will heal miraculously. The bullets inside your body will be pushed out by regenerating muscle. Don't forget, this is a super anti-aging serum and a cell-revitalizing elixir!"

My hands suddenly grabbed the bamboo container, and I brought it to my lips. I was about to taste the milky liquid.

But at that moment, a thought struck me: once I started drinking this liquid, I would have to keep drinking it.

And if I went without it for a period of time, I would turn into an idiot, a living corpse!

This terrifying consequence made me hesitate, but not for long.

Because in my current situation, I didn't have the luxury of deliberation.

If I didn't drink the "elixir of immortality," I would lose consciousness within ten minutes, and death would follow.

But if I drank it, despite the potential consequences, I would at least survive for now.

I opened my mouth wide and gulped down the elixir, one mouthful after another. The elixir was cold, but as it went down, it created a burning sensation, like strong liquor.

I drank the entire half-tube of the elixir, and soon, a dizzying sensation overwhelmed me. My vision blurred, and I felt like a drunkard.

The sea and sky seemed to merge into one, indistinguishable. Everything around me faded, and I felt as if my body had become light and soft, floating upward.

Gradually, it felt like my body no longer existed. I seemed to dissolve into a mist, blending with the hazy sea and sky.

I wanted to check how my wounds had changed after drinking the elixir, but when I looked down, I couldn't see my own body!

Not being able to see one's own body is something only people with severe mental disorders experience. They might scream, "Where are my hands?

Where are my feet?" even though their limbs are perfectly intact—they just can't see them.

Had my brain been damaged, turning me into an incurable madman?

But I knew that wasn't the case. I wouldn't go mad. Even though I couldn't see my body at the moment, my mind was still clear. I remembered everything that had happened.

I closed my eyes and let time slip away. After what felt like an eternity, I began to feel my body descending, as if I were slowly floating down from the clouds.

Finally, my back touched something solid again.

I opened my eyes and saw Mark first. He was tossing his gun in his hand, seemingly no longer hostile toward me.

I quickly checked my body. The wounds were completely gone, as if I had never been shot.

But I *had* been shot.

My memory confirmed it, and the bloodstains on my clothes were proof.

I struggled to stand up, still feeling a bit lightheaded, but I soon steadied myself. Mark looked at me and asked, "How do you feel?"

I shook my head vigorously, trying to determine if I was dreaming. I was fully awake—this wasn't a dream.

But the hazy sensation I had experienced after drinking the elixir was hard to recall. I forced a bitter smile and didn't answer.

Mark laughed heartily. "Feeling amazing, aren't you? Honestly, it's just like the high from heroin, isn't it?"

He asked "isn't it?" twice, and I had no choice but to nod.

Because what he said was true.

Mark was clearly pleased with himself, gesturing animatedly. "I believe the natives on that island originally used this liquid as a narcotic. Throughout history, people have always been drawn to narcotics—and you'll soon grow to love this too!"

In that moment, I felt a chill run through my body.

I had drunk the elixir of immortality.

I would no longer be able to live without the elixir. If I stopped drinking it, the anti-aging serum's side effects would turn me into an idiot!

I stood there, frozen, while Mark watched me with a grin. After a while, he said, "Don't be so down. Come on, let's shake hands. We can be the best partners!"

He extended his hand, and I could easily have grabbed it and thrown him into the sea. But I didn't. What would be the point?

I had already drunk the elixir. I was now its prisoner. From this moment on, I had no freedom.

Mark's joy and his belief that I would cooperate with him stemmed from his understanding of this fact. Of course, I didn't throw him into the sea, but I also didn't shake his hand.

In my mind, I reflected on the countless enemies I had encountered during my years of bizarre adventures. Some were dangerous, some cunning, and some were simply indescribable.

But among all the enemies I had faced, none were as formidable as Mark. Time and again, I had failed against him, and now it seemed there was no way to turn the tables.

Seeing that I refused to shake his hand, Mark withdrew it and shrugged. "Whether you like it or not, I don't see any other path for you."

Gradually, my mind regained its composure. "I could still send you back to face the electric chair."

Mark continued to smile. "No, you won't. You've drunk the elixir. Contrary to what most people think, an immortal person is far from happy. Their heart is filled with bitterness, emptiness, and loneliness. The thought of never dying can send shivers down your spine. I'm not wrong, am I? I've hit the nail on the head, haven't I?"

My body trembled involuntarily.

Mark was right again!

In the past, if I had thought about immortality, I might have found it intriguing, even enviable. Back then, it was just a fantasy, and everything seemed perfect. But now it was different.

Now, as long as I kept drinking the elixir, I could truly become immortal. But every time I thought about it, I couldn't help but feel a chill.

When you and your loved ones grow old together, it doesn't feel so bad. But imagine watching everyone around you, including your dearest loved ones, age and die while you remain unchanged. Could that be called happiness? It's utterly horrifying!

Mark looked at me and said slowly, "Isn't it?"

"Isn't it?" seemed to be his catchphrase. I just stared at him listlessly.

Mark continued, "Spiritually, we are far from happy. Someone in this state always hopes to find another person in the same situation, someone to share their misery and offer comfort. I'm like that, and so are you!"

He paused before concluding, "That's why you won't send me back to face the electric chair."

I still had nothing to say.

I remained silent because he was right. If I were alone, the emptiness in my heart would only grow. Having someone to share this burden would make it more bearable.

But I'm also a fiercely independent person. When I realized Mark was using this to control me, I instinctively wanted to counter his argument.

After a long pause, I sneered, "You're mistaken. Of course, I need someone who shares my fate, but why should I choose you?"

I expected Mark to be shocked by my words, but instead, he laughed heartily, doubling over with such force that the canoe nearly capsized.

I shouted, "What are you laughing at?"

Mark replied, "You've thought it through, but you've overlooked two things. First, if I can't avoid the electric chair, I'll reveal everything before I die. Think about it—what would happen then?"

I couldn't help but shudder.

Indeed, if Mark revealed everything, I would become completely different from everyone else. People would see me as a monster, and my life would be worse than that of a death row inmate!

Mark sneered, "Do you know why I pushed my brother off the cliff? When I told him everything, he said he would announce it to the world. He might not have meant any harm, but I was terrified, so I pushed him!"

These words finally cleared up one of the mysteries in my mind—why Mark had killed Brian. But of course, many other questions remained, such as the mistaken identity after the incident or Luna Xi's attitude. However, in my current state, I wasn't in the mood to press him further.

Mark sneered again and said, "Second, you've overlooked something even more important—you have no choice!"

I was puzzled by his words, but then he pointed toward the sea. I followed his gaze and saw a small submarine surfacing from the water.

Only then did I realize that Mark had indeed used a radio to contact the submarine.

CHAPTER 11

Will I Become an Idiot?

The submarine was an old model, a relic from World War II, but judging by how smoothly it surfaced, it was clearly still in excellent condition.

As the submarine emerged close to us, the waves it created rocked the canoe violently, nearly throwing both Mark and me into the sea. This could have been a perfect opportunity for me to jump into the water and escape, but could I really outrun a submarine?

After a brief moment of consideration, I dismissed the idea.

Soon, the entire submarine surfaced, and the hatch opened, revealing the upper half of a man. He was a thin Japanese man.

Mark waved at the Japanese man. "Return to the control room. I need to bring a friend aboard."

The Japanese man quickly retreated inside. Mark paddled the canoe closer to the submarine. "You first."

I didn't jump onto the submarine immediately. Instead, I asked, "What exactly do you want me to do?"

Mark smiled while playing with the gun in his hand, clearly trying to intimidate me. He said, "We can discuss the details inside the submarine. Go on."

I stared at his gun for a moment. The barrel was pointed directly at my heart. If I didn't want to get shot and end up as shark food, I had no choice but to obey.

I leaped onto the submarine's deck, and he continued to point the gun at me. I climbed into the hatch, and Mark followed.

It was a small submarine, one of the smallest models from its time. During World War II, such submarines weren't used for combat but for communication or transporting agents. It could hold no more than five people.

Despite its size, operating this submarine alone required exceptional skill. The Japanese man must have been a mechanical genius.

Once inside, Mark forced me into the submarine's only cabin. We sat on the bunk beds, and he kept his gun trained on me, maintaining a safe distance.

My mind was in chaos, but I managed to ask, "What exactly are you planning to do with me?"

Mark replied, "I want you to join my plan."

I said coldly, "Selling the elixir in bottles?"

"Yes, but that's the final step. First, you must return with me to Han Tong Jia Island and kill all the natives—every single one of them!"

My body trembled violently, and I shouted, "Nonsense! Do you think I'm as crazy as you?"

Mark sneered, "But you don't have to pretend to be a saint. Haven't you killed before? The most recent example is Poggin—you killed him."

I retorted immediately, "That's completely different! Poggin was a criminal, but the natives on the island—"

Mark cut me off with a wave of his hand. "Enough! Even if Poggin was a criminal, who are you? A judge? Is your opinion the law? What gives you the right to sentence him to death and act as the executioner?"

Mark's rapid-fire questions left me speechless!

I had always said that, in my years of adventurous life, I had encountered all kinds of opponents, but none as formidable as Mark.

However, at this moment, I had to admit that Mark's wit and intelligence were not only on par with mine but possibly even superior.

While I was in a daze, Mark sneered, "It's okay if you don't want to do it. I can do it alone. Killing them all won't be a loss. What's the difference between living like that and dying?"

My breathing quickened as I saw Mark's expression. He wasn't just talking—he was serious. How could I not be shocked?

Mark was planning to massacre the peaceful natives on this serene island. No one in the world was as calm and irrational as him.

I thought rapidly. If I could take the gun from his hand, maybe I could prevent this horrific massacre.

But Mark anticipated my thoughts. Before I could act, he stood up, stepped back, opened the door, and flashed out. His movements were swift. Before I could react, he had already retreated out of the cabin.

The gun in his hand was still pointed at my heart. "You'd better not think of anything else. I was the all-around shooting champion in the army. If you don't cooperate, your life means nothing to me."

I was stunned. His words were clear. If I resisted, he no longer needed me and would kill me!

As soon as he finished speaking, he closed the cabin door with a "bang."

I rushed forward. The door was locked from the outside. I pushed hard, but it wouldn't budge.

I looked around for something to pry the door open. I didn't know what to do even if I pried it open, but I had to try.

I found a pair of pointed pliers and pried and hit the door hard, making "bang bang" sounds.

Despite all the noise I made, there was no reaction. The hull's shaking told me the submarine was sinking into the sea.

Mark had begun his plan. He intended to go to Han Tong Jia Island and kill all the natives—people who had once saved him and had no intention of harming him.

I had to act, but I was powerless in this situation.

I kept knocking on the door and shouting. After half an hour, the hatch opened. I rushed out, but was struck hard on the back of my head.

My vision went dark, and I fell heavily to the ground.

I was knocked unconscious by the blow.

The darkness enveloped me like a suffocating shroud, yet my mind burned with an unnatural clarity—a cruel gift, perhaps, of the elixir I had consumed. My body lay utterly paralyzed, a mere husk devoid of sight, sound, or sensation, yet my consciousness remained razor-sharp, a cruel paradox that sent icy tendrils of dread through the very fabric of my being. It was as though my essence had been violently wrenched from its mortal shell, leaving behind an empty vessel while my soul drifted, unmoored, in a vast and silent void.

But the soul is blind and deaf, unable to feel anything. Initially, the sensation is strange, but the absence of feeling quickly turns to pain and terror, as if bound tightly in a dark, sunless cellar.

My thoughts remained clear despite the fear. I told myself this was temporary – I had fainted. The super anti-aging hormones I had taken must have stimulated my brain cells, allowing me to continue thinking even after losing consciousness.

Time became meaningless in this limbo. I had no way of knowing how long I'd been unconscious or what my companion Mark might be doing to my helpless form. The complete sensory void made every moment an exercise in psychological endurance.

Then, like a thunderclap in the silent void, sound came crashing back into my world. At first distant and muffled, the screams pierced through my consciousness - raw, primal shrieks of terror and agony that grew louder with each passing second. As my hearing sharpened, I realized the source was terrifyingly close.

The cacophony of horror escalated - not just screams now, but the staccato rhythm of gunfire and the high-pitched whine of bullets cutting through the air.

My pulse raced as adrenaline flooded my system, every nerve ending screaming danger. Against my better judgment, I forced my eyes open.

What greeted me was a scene so horrifying that my body froze in primal terror. My eyes refused to obey my frantic mental commands to close, locked wide open by sheer shock.

The grotesque tableau before me defied comprehension, momentarily short-circuiting my ability to process the nightmare unfolding mere feet away. In that moment, I would have given anything to return to the peaceful oblivion of sensory deprivation.

I had never witnessed such madness and cruelty. Mark held a portable machine gun, firing relentlessly. Bullets flew into the bodies of the natives. Normally, they would only die if shot in the heart.

But Mark didn't need to aim. He fired wildly, and each native was hit with at least 20 bullets.

Among so many bullets, one always found its mark. The open space was filled with dead bodies. A dozen natives, not fatally shot, stood there in shock.

They had no intention of resisting. They didn't know what to do.

It didn't take long before they too fell.

The gunshots stopped. Mark's hand retracted from the trigger, and he wiped his sweat. But I still heard the "da da" sound in my ears.

It was an illusion, born from the deep and unforgettable impression of this horrific incident.

It took a long time before I could breathe. My panting caught Mark's attention. He turned, grinning with wolf-like teeth, "How is it?"

I was so agitated I could hardly speak. "You are a... a..."

Before I could find the right word, he pointed the gun at me. I shouted,

"You are a crazy beast!"

Mark pulled the trigger again!

But his hand sank, causing the muzzle to tilt upward. More than ten bullets whizzed over my head.

I stood up and approached him. My expression must have been terrifying because he looked horrified and screamed, "What do you want?"

I rushed forward, jumped in front of him, and shouted, "I want to kill you!"

He raised the machine gun to smash it down at me, but I was faster. My fist sank heavily into his abdomen. The force was strong. Mark may not have felt the pain, but he couldn't avoid twitching. His body bent down, and the strength in his hand disappeared.

When his machine gun hit me, I didn't feel much pain. I didn't stop. As his body bent down, my knee hit his chin heavily.

When his portable machine gun hit me, I didn't feel any pain. I didn't stop. As he bent down, I raised my knee and hit his chin.

He let out a strange cry, threw away the gun, and fell with his back to the sky. I immediately pounced on him and pinned him down.

If Mark's action of killing the natives was crazy, then my action was almost as crazy.

I used both hands to tightly pinch his neck. The force was so great that my hands lost consciousness. There was only one thought in my heart: I must strangle him to death!

The force in my hands grew stronger. I had never used such strength before. I believed it could break an iron pipe as thick as his neck!

His neck bones began to crackle, his hands waved wildly, his feet kicked, but after five minutes, his struggle gradually stopped.

He opened his mouth wide, his tongue exposed, his eyes bulging—his appearance was terrifying.

When I saw this, I first thought: he is dead. But then I thought, he will not die.

These thoughts made my mind clearer. I realized he couldn't die now, which would be extremely disadvantageous to me.

When I thought of this, my hands suddenly loosened, and my body fell to the ground.

I had exerted too much force and couldn't stand up. Mark lay there, his bulging eyes staring at me like a dead fish. He didn't move, so I couldn't tell if he was dead or alive. I took a few breaths and struggled to stand. My eyes remained on his face. After a while, his eyes slowly turned. He was alive!

His eyeballs moved faster, and his chest began to rise and fall. In a dry, unpleasant voice, he said, "You almost strangled me!"

He survived. Anyone else would have died under such pressure, but Mark survived like a miracle.

It seemed that unless his head and body were separated, he couldn't die. He supported himself on the ground and sat up.

His expression returned to normal, and he stood up. "You almost strangled me to death!" he repeated.

I took a breath and said, "I will still strangle you to death."

He let out a bitter chuckle, staggering forward two unsteady steps. "It seems cooperation is beyond us," he muttered.

As he spoke, he continued to advance. I wasn't sure what his intentions were, so I simply watched him in silence. But then, in a flash, I realized what he was about to do.

In that same instant, Mark's movements became a blur of speed. But I was already in motion, leaping forward with equal urgency. He lunged for the machine gun, his fingers closing around it just as my feet came down hard on his hand.

The force of my landing forced him to release his grip. With a swift kick, I sent the gun skittering across the ground and bolted forward. Mark was quick to give chase, but his movements were always half a step behind mine. By the time he caught up, I already had the gun in my hands.

I leveled the weapon at him, my voice cold and steady. "Don't move. Even if you were raised on the elixir of immortality, one pull of this trigger, and you're finished."

Mark froze, two yards away, his chest heaving. "What do you want?" he demanded.

"First, I'm taking you back. Then I'll notify the authorities to head to Timor Island and find Luna Xi," I replied.

Mark's eyes narrowed. "You think you can just walk away?"

I glanced at the scattered bodies lying lifeless on the ground. "Of course," I said. "What else would you expect me to do?"

The tension hung thick in the air, the weight of the moment pressing down like a storm about to break.

He spoke slowly, his voice dripping with a chilling calm. "It makes no difference to me. If I go back, death is inevitable. But you—how much of the elixir do you plan to take with you? I could suggest you take more, but how much can you carry? Even if you could take every last drop, it will run out eventually. And then what? Do you know how to make more? Do you even understand the process?"

He fired off a barrage of questions, each one sharper than the last. I stood there, silent, unable to answer a single one.

A faint, mocking smile crept across his lips. "I think you're starting to see the truth. Without you, I can find another partner. I can survive just fine. But without me? You're nothing."

His words struck like a dagger to the heart. I hesitated, then took a few steps back, my eyes scanning the lifeless bodies around us. I bent down and untied a bamboo flask from the waist of a fallen tribesman. Without thinking, I tilted my head back and drank deeply from it—the so-called "elixir of immortality."

I couldn't explain why I did it. It was instinctive, like a smoker reaching for a cigarette in a moment of weakness.

Mark let out a guttural laugh, his voice dripping with triumph. "See? I was right, wasn't I?"

I spun around, the gun still clenched in my hand. "Don't think for a second that you've got me cornered. I'm still taking you back. You *will* face execution."

His smile vanished, replaced by a look of sheer desperation. His face turned ashen. "You're insane," he spat. "Have you no sense of self-preservation? Let me make this clear—every tribesman here is dead. I'm the only one left who knows how to make the elixir."

I took a deep breath, steadying myself. "Don't worry. I won't beg you to reveal the secret."

Truth be told, I had no clear plan for what lay ahead. My future was a foggy, uncertain void. But one thing was certain: I *would* bring Mark back.

I grabbed a large bamboo flask from one of the tribesmen and tossed it to him. Then I selected another of equal size, filled with the same mysterious liquid, and slung it over my shoulder.

With the gun still trained on him, I barked, "Move!"

Mark stared at me, his eyes wide and unyielding. He was clearly making one last attempt to sway me. "Think carefully," he said, his voice low and urgent. "If you do this, you'll be signing your own death warrant. You'll become a fool—a shell of yourself."

My resolve was ironclad, unshakable. "Don't waste your breath worrying about me," I said coldly. "I know what I'm doing. Save your concern for yourself."

Mark's face darkened, his expression more ominous than the storm clouds gathering overhead. He turned slowly, his back to me, and stood there for a moment, as if weighing his options. Then, with a reluctant step, he began to walk forward. I followed close behind, my gun trained on him.

The walk to the beach was a blur of chaos in my mind. I pushed aside thoughts of what might have been—what could have been—and focused solely on the task at hand. Once we reached the shore, I knew the submarine would be our only way off this cursed island. But the question remained: who would pilot it?

If I left the task to the Japanese man, I'd have to contend with two adversaries during the long journey. That was a complication I couldn't afford. I had some knowledge of submarine navigation—enough to get by. If I took control myself, the problem would simplify significantly.

By the time we neared the beach, I had already made up my mind. When the Japanese man approached, I barked an order: "You! Head to the center of the island!"

He stared at me, confusion etched across his face. Then, like a cat bristling with fury, his shoulders hunched, and for a moment, I thought he might lunge at me. But his eyes flicked to the gun in my hand, and he thought better of it. Without a word, he turned and strode toward the heart of the island.

The Japanese man remained silent, but Mark wasn't so restrained. He let out a strangled cry. "Are you insane? Do you even know how to operate a submarine?"

I didn't dignify his question with a response. Instead, I pressed the barrel of the gun firmly into his back, urging him forward. "Keep moving," I said, my voice low and steady. "We're not done yet."

The weight of the moment hung heavy in the air, the tension between us crackling like the storm about to break. But I didn't falter. I had made my choice, and there was no turning back.

We reached the shoreline, the submarine resting ominously just offshore. My previous failure at Mark's hands had taught me caution. Without warning, I flipped the gun in my hand and struck him hard on the back of the head with the butt.

He crumpled to the ground without a sound. I quickly gathered some wild vines and bound his hands and feet tightly, then hoisted his unconscious body over my shoulder and made my way to the submarine.

The irony wasn't lost on me. When I had first arrived on this island, I had been unconscious, carried by Mark. Now, the tables had turned. He was the one knocked out, and I was the one in control. A faint sense of triumph flickered in my chest—victory, at least for now, was mine.

I shoved Mark's limp form through the hatch and followed him inside. I locked him in one of the cabins, leaving a bamboo flask of the elixir beside him. Then I made my way to the control room, where I began inspecting the machinery.

The submarine was old, but I was confident I could navigate it. To my relief, the communication equipment was in perfect working order. Once I cleared the turbulent waters, I could send out a distress signal.

I guided the submarine away from the shore and submerged it, steering cautiously through the underwater currents. The turbulence was fierce, the vessel rocking violently like a cradle caught in a storm. For a moment, I feared it might flip over and never right itself.

But my fears were unfounded. The submarine soon stabilized, and I managed to bring it to the surface. Without hesitation, I activated the radio and sent out a distress call.

The response was quicker than I had dared to hope. Within an hour, an Australian naval vessel had acknowledged my signal.

Six hours later, as the sun dipped below the horizon, painting the sea in hues of crimson and gold, Mark and I were aboard the warship.

The ship's commander, a seasoned admiral, inspected the special credentials issued to me by Interpol. I explained that Mark was a condemned prisoner who needed to be returned to face justice, and that I was his escort. The admiral asked no further questions and promised to deliver us to the nearest port as quickly as possible.

True to his word, within twenty-four hours, we were on land and boarding a plane. Before takeoff, I fulfilled a promise I had made to myself: I called Flora. Her voice trembled with emotion, a mix of tears and relief, as I told her I was coming home.

By noon on the third day, I arrived back with Mark in custody. To my surprise, waiting at the airport were not only Flora but also Jack, the head of the police special operations unit.

Jack's disappointment was palpable. He had clearly hoped I'd never return, let alone with Mark in tow. But he forced a hearty laugh, masking his frustration with feigned enthusiasm.

Mark was promptly handed over to the authorities and taken away.

And so, it seemed, the ordeal was over. But there are a few critical details that must be addressed—details that cannot be overlooked. Pay close attention, especially to the final point.

Here are the key points that need to be addressed:

1. **Mark Xi's Execution**: Mark Xi was swiftly executed upon his return. His story ended with the finality of death, a fitting conclusion for a man who had manipulated life and death for his own gain.

2. **Luna Xi's Fate:** Luna Xi, stranded on Timor Island, had become a shell of her former self—a victim of the elixir's cruel dependency. Without a steady supply, her mind had deteriorated into a state of irreversible stupor. She had known the truth— that her husband had died in the fall, and that Mark Xi was his brother. But her cunning, her greed, had blinded her. She had conspired with Mark Xi, believing she could become the wealthiest woman in the world. Instead, she was left with nothing but shattered dreams.

3. **The Disappearance of Han Tong Jia Island:** Three months after my return, a small, barely noticed news item caught my attention. It reported a

strange and sudden tsunami in the South Pacific, suggesting that an island had sunk due to tectonic shifts. The location was remote, and no one had ever officially documented an island there. The area was notorious for its treacherous waves, making it impossible to investigate thoroughly. Aerial surveys revealed nothing but calm waters and a few scattered debris floating on the surface. I knew then that Han Tong Jia Island had vanished beneath the waves. With it, the miraculous plant that produced the anti-aging elixir—the so-called "immortality drug"—was lost forever. The secret of eternal youth had been swallowed by the ocean.

4. **My Own Predicament:** Finally, there's the matter of my own condition. After reuniting with Flora, I had no choice but to confess everything about the elixir. I sought out some of the world's most renowned endocrinologists and internal medicine specialists, explaining the bizarre effects of the drug on my body. They agreed to treat me, devising a daily regimen of complex procedures designed to suppress the overactive glands responsible for the excessive production of anti-aging hormones. The goal was to restore my body's natural balance. But they warned me that if

the suppression therapy failed, they would have to perform an intricate and risky surgery to remove certain glands.

The endocrine system remains one of the most enigmatic frontiers of medical science. Even these experts admitted that they were venturing into uncharted territory. Could they successfully remove the overactive glands without causing catastrophic side effects? And if they did, what unforeseen consequences would I face? The human body is a delicate machine, and tampering with its inner workings is never without risk.

Even though the experts overseeing my treatment were among the best in their fields, they still required me to sign a consent form—a document that felt more like a surrender to fate than a medical formality.

As I scrawled my name across the bottom, a bitter laugh echoed in my mind. What had I become? A guinea pig in a high-stakes experiment, a man teetering on the edge of an abyss, unsure whether he would emerge whole or broken.

I could only imagine the anguish Flora must have been feeling.

She was a pillar of strength, never allowing a hint of sorrow to surface in my presence. Instead, she offered constant encouragement, her voice steady, her smile unwavering. But I knew her too well. Beneath that calm exterior, her heart was a storm. When we were together, her fingers would twist and knot, betraying the tension she fought so hard to conceal. All I could do was reach out and hold her hand, a feeble attempt to offer comfort in the face of an uncertain future.

It was a quiet tragedy, one I can barely bring myself to dwell on.

The truth is, no one—not even the experts—could guarantee the outcome of my treatment. The road ahead was long and fraught with uncertainty. I was to be isolated, cut off from the world, confined to a state of rest and recovery. The question loomed large: Would I emerge from this ordeal unscathed, or would I be forever altered?

But then, perhaps there's no need to worry. After all, I am the protagonist of this serialized tale, and protagonists have a way of escaping the jaws of disaster, don't they? No matter how dire the circumstances, they always find a way to turn the tide, to emerge victorious against all odds. So, rest assured, dear reader—this story is far from over. Whatever challenges lie ahead, I will face them head-on, and I will prevail.

Because that's what heroes do.